3/28

Santa in
Montana

**Center Point
Large Print**

Also by Janet Dailey
and available from Center Point Large Print:

Santa in a Stetson

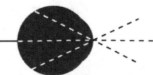

**This Large Print Book carries the
Seal of Approval of N.A.V.H.**

Santa in Montana

Janet Dailey

CENTER POINT PUBLISHING
THORNDIKE, MAINE

This Center Point Large Print edition
is published in the year 2010 by arrangement with
Kensington Publishing Corp.

The text of this Large Print edition is unabridged.
In other aspects, this book may vary
from the original edition.
Printed in the United States of America
on permanent paper.
Set in 16-point Times New Roman type.

ISBN: 978-1-60285-900-5

Library of Congress Cataloging-in-Publication Data

Dailey, Janet.
Santa in Montana / Janet Dailey.
   p. cm.
ISBN 978-1-60285-900-5 (lib. bdg. : alk. paper)
1. Christmas stories. 2. Large type books. I. Title.
PS3554.A29S275 2010
813'.54—dc22

2010028746

In memory of my Bill,
who warned me not to use
the word "never"

And to all the readers who asked if I
couldn't please write just one
more Calder story

Chapter 1

A chinook wind, long known as the snow-eater by native tribes, swept across the vast Montana plains. Its breath was warm, melting the wintry white blanket that covered the land's rich grasses.

Over the undulating land of the high prairie it raced and soon invaded the headquarters of the famed Triple C ranch, swirling around the many buildings that gave the place the semblance of a small town. Inevitably the chinook swung up the hillock and tunneled through the tall columns lining the porch of the big white house that held a commanding view of the ranch yard. Its next target was the smoke curling from the chimney, flattening it off and carrying it along on its race over the land. The source of the smoke was the fire that blazed in the den's massive stone fireplace. Its heat was a concession to the Triple C's aging patriarch, Chase Calder. He sat in his usual chair behind the room's big oak desk, his cane hooked on the edge of it. The years had taken much of his vigor, just as it had shrunken his big frame and carved a network of deep lines in his rawboned face. But nothing had dulled the sharp gleam in his deep set eyes. Old, Chase Calder might be, but only a fool would think that age had diminished his awareness of the things happening around him.

His glance wandered to his widowed daughter-in-law. Jessy Calder sat in one of the wingbacked chairs facing the desk. Dressed in typical ranch garb of cowboy boots, jeans, and a shirt, she still possessed the boy-slim figure of her youth. Only the attractive age lines around the eyes and the slight silvering of her nut-brown hair revealed that Jessy, too, had grown older. Currently the reins of the Triple C were in her hands. That she held them with ease spoke both to Chase's quiet tutelage and to her own innate ability.

Like many other ranch hands, her roots were sunk deep in the land. She'd been born on the ranch, and her early years spent as an ordinary cowhand before marrying Chase's only son. Her solid knowledge of the cattle business and her abiding respect for the land that supported it, coupled with her own quiet strength, provided the basis for a sound leader.

Of late, Jessy had turned more of the responsibility for the ranch's daily operations over to her son Trey, preparing him for the day when he would take control just as Chase had prepared her. It was this freedom from the day-to-day minutiae that allowed Jessy to relax in the den and enjoy a mid-morning cup of coffee with her father-in-law.

A particular strong wind gust briefly rattled one of the window panes. Automatically Jessy glanced in its direction, pausing in the act of raising the coffee cup to her lips.

"I like the sound of that," she remarked idly. "It means we won't have to hay the cattle. The longer they have good Calder grass to graze, the better off our bottom line will be."

Even as the glimmer of a confirming smile deepened the corners of Chase's mouth, the tall lanky cowboy standing by the fireplace sent a sideways smile in Jessy's direction. "Spoken like a true cattleman." The observation came from Laredo Smith, a suggestion of a drawl in his voice that pegged him as coming from someplace well south of Montana. "Now, me, I was thinking about how muddy the ground would be at the Boar's Nest. When this ground thaws, it turns to gumbo."

The Boar's Nest was the name given to an old-line shack on the Triple C that Laredo called home—and where he and Jessy had stolen many pleasurable moments.

An amused chuckle slipped from her, its warmth matching the gleam of love that was in the look she gave him. "After all this time, we still haven't made a real cowhand out of you, have we, Laredo?"

"Not for the want of trying." His blues held an answering twinkle.

It was the kind of look that was exchanged between lovers. Just for a moment, Chase had the feeling he was intruding. At the same time it reminded him of the way his late wife Maggie used to look at him. She'd been gone from this world for half a lifetime, but the love he felt for her was as deep and strong as ever. It was something Chase never talked about, abiding instead by the unwritten code of the Old West that insisted a man's grief was a private thing.

Outside the telltale rumble of a vehicle's engine made itself heard in the den. Chase lifted his head in mild curiosity. "Sounds like someone just drove up."

Turning, Laredo glanced out the front window. "It's a state patrol car."

"Really. I wonder why they're here." It was curiosity rather than concern that prompted Jessy to stand and absently set her cup down.

"I'm guessing you'll soon find out," Laredo replied as the muffled thud of a car door closing penetrated the den. "I'll go make sure there's a fresh pot of coffee brewing in the kitchen."

Chase watched the long-legged cowboy make his exit from the room. "He's never broke the habit of playing it safe, has he?" he remarked to Jessy.

"I doubt he ever will." She made the matter-of-fact response with a shrug of her shoulder and exited the room to greet the arriving officer at the front door.

The exchange was a rare acknowledgment of their mutual awareness that the man they knew as Laredo Smith had a past that didn't bear close scrutiny. Their lack of concern was another example of the old western codes in play, specifically the one that insisted a man be judged as he stood before them and not for what he might—or might not have done—before they knew him.

From the front entry came modulated voices exchanging pleasantries. It was soon followed by the sound of two sets of footsteps approaching the den. Jessy walked through the doorway accompanied by a uniformed trooper, his heavy jacket unzipped but not abandoned, a sure sign his visit would likely be a short one.

"This is Trooper Van Fleet," Jessy told Chase by way of an introduction, then addressed the patrolman. "I believe you know my father-in-law, Chase Calder."

"Of course. Good to see you again." Gloveless, the trooper reached across the desk to briefly shake hands.

Chase came straight to the point. "Is this a business or social cause?"

"A bit of both," the man acknowledged, then added wryly, "At least, it's business of a sort. I know we're still a couple days away from Thanksgiving, but we're trying to get an early jump on Christmas. You see, this year we're joining with the Marines in their Toys for Tots campaign. Naturally we'd like to enlist the support of the Triple C if we can."

"It's a worthy cause," Chase stated. "Especially now when so many people are having hard times."

Sidetracked by his own comment, Chase thought about all the economic downturns—some more severe than others—that the Triple C had survived in its nearly century and a half existence. He had no doubt it would weather this one as well, thanks to the careful management of the woman in charge, but that didn't make him indifferent to the hardships of others.

He nodded ever so slightly at his daughter-in-law. As always, Chase delegated any final decision to Jessy, confident she would readily agree to have the Triple C participate in the toy drive.

After taking a seat in the second wingback chair, the trooper proceeded to explain everything from the ultimate goal to the timetable and logistics of the campaigning. Such mundane yet essential details failed to hold Chase's attention, even less so when he recognized the light footfalls outside the door. Mere seconds later his daughter Cat entered the den, an insulated coffee carafe and extra cups balanced on the tray she carried.

Petite in frame, Cat was the image of her late mother, possessing the same green eyes and midnight dark hair. She wore her hair shorter than Maggie had. When Chase had once commented on the haircut Cat had been quick to assert it was

12

easy to care for and chic. Privately Chase acknowledged it was flattering and made her appear much younger than she was.

Chase watched with a father's pride as the trooper promptly stood upon Cat's entrance. "Mrs. Echohawk." He spoke her name with open respect. "It's a pleasure to see you today."

For a short moment, Cat's gaze made an examination of his face. Then a faint smile of recognition touched her lips. "We met at the sheriff's office," she recalled. "Trooper Van Fleet, isn't it?"

"Yes, ma'am." He looked pleased that she remembered his name.

Her smile widened. "Welcome to the Triple C." She set the tray atop the desk and picked up the insulated serving pot. "Would you like some coffee? It's fresh."

"Love some."

"I've never known a man in uniform to turn down a cup." Cat smiled as she handed him a full one.

"True enough," he admitted, hesitated, then added a bit self-consciously, "I had the pleasure of working with your late husband on several occasions. Logan was a good sheriff and a good man."

"Thank you," Cat replied, but this was a household that didn't talk about personal grief.

Before the moment could become awkward,

Jessy spoke up, "Trooper Van Fleet is here on behalf of the Marines' Toys for Tots campaign."

"I was hoping this was a social call," Cat admitted, then smiled a little ruefully. "Christmas—it's not very far off, is it?"

"Just over a month." Cup in hand, the officer returned to his seat in the wingback.

"And that will go by fast," Cat murmured, then turned to Jessy. "Want a refill?"

"Sure." She held out her cup and waited while Cat poured more.

"Might as well top mine off while you're here." Chase pushed his cup forward.

"Sorry, Dad, but this is the real stuff," Cat informed him. "I'll come back with your decaf."

"Save yourself the trip to the kitchen and just fill my cup with what you've got in the pot," Chase stated.

"Now, Dad," she began.

But Chase cut across her words before she could complete her admonition. "My daughter likes to think she knows what's best for me." He directed the comment to the officer, the coolness of his voice clearly indicating his opinion of it.

"You know you're supposed to cut back on the caffeine, Dad," Cat reminded him.

"There are a lot of things I'm supposed to do that I don't. Now, fill my cup." The latter statement had the familiar bark of a man accustomed to being obeyed.

14

Lips pressed tightly together in disapproval, Cat poured coffee into his cup, then attempted to reassume her role as hostess by turning to the trooper. "I didn't ask whether you take cream or sugar. I have both on the tray."

"Black is fine," he assured her, then took several folded together papers out of an inside pocket and handed them to Jessy. "I printed out everything you'd need to know. We really appreciate you signing on. The support of the Triple C will mean a lot."

"Glad to help," Jessy replied and laid the papers on the desk. "I'll read them later."

With all the curiosity of her nickname, Cat snuck a look at the papers. "You're partnering with the Toys for Tots this year. That's good to hear."

"No one likes to see kids go without—at any time of year." Something in his tone implied that he'd seen more of it than he wanted.

Chase didn't allow the conversation to get mired in the current economic troubles. "Every time parents have to tighten their belts, Santa's bag just gets bigger—like it will this year."

Everyone smiled in agreement, and the talk centered around the current campaign. Once the trooper finished his coffee, he didn't linger, pleading other stops to make. Cat saw him to the door.

"I'll spread the word about the toy drive—and

15

make sure it's posted at the ranch store," Jessy said, idly speaking her thoughts. "Mom would be good at organizing this. She was complaining the other day that she needed some kind of project."

"Stumpy will appreciate that," Chase commented, referring to her father. "He told me just the other day she was turning into a royal nag."

Laredo returned to the den in time to hear the latter remark. "Are you talking about Cat again?"

"The shoe does fit her too, but in this case, we were referring to Jessy's mother," Chase answered.

"I think I'll just forget I heard anything." Laredo helped himself to another cup of coffee and glanced in the direction of the front window as the patrol car pulled away.

The verifying glance didn't escape Chase's notice. But he didn't comment on it, just as he didn't say anything about Laredo's return coming on the heels of the trooper's departure. Instead he simply took a sip of his own coffee. Cat paused in the doorway, drawing his glance.

"Did you want something, Cat?"

As she opened her mouth to reply, the quiet of the house was shattered by the sound of boot-clumping feet and a little boy's voice calling, "Greypa! Greypa!"

"In here, Jake," Chase called out needlessly as his four-year-old great-grandson charged into the den, nearly mowing Cat down in the process.

Chase swung his swivel chair around to face the young boy who came barreling around the desk to him, his chin jutting out to match the fixed look of determination on his face, an expression almost shockingly familiar to the one that Chase had been known to wear in the past. Bending forward, Chase ran an inspecting glance over the scarf-like head covering the boy wore. It sat slightly askew despite the encircling black band that was intended to hold it in place.

He fought back a smile and asked, "What's the problem, son?"

"It's Mom," Jake declared and clamped his mouth shut in a mutinous line.

As if on cue, his mother Sloan entered the room. A mingling of amusement and exasperation rippled across her face when she located her son behind the desk.

"What about your mom?" Chase wanted to know.

"She says I can't wear my cowboy boots in the Christmas play. She says I have to wear sandals. I don't, do I?" Jake insisted, confident he had an ally in his great-grandfather.

"You're supposed to be a shepherd boy, aren't you?"

His brow furrowed in an unhappy frown. "Yeah, but . . ."

"No buts, Jake." Chase held up a silencing

hand. "Let me explain it this way, if Jesus had been born here on the Triple C, cowboys would have come to worship Him in their cowboy boots. But Jesus was born in Bethlehem. So shepherds knelt before Him, and they wore sandals."

"Sandals are for girls, Greypa," Jake protested, using the name he had coined for him when he first began to talk and couldn't wrap his tongue around a mouthful like great-grandpa.

"Girls and shepherd boys. Right?" The single-word question challenged the boy to agree.

Jake heaved a big, disgruntled sigh. "Right."

From the doorway, Sloan marveled, "I don't know how you do it, Chase. I've gone around and around with him over this issue of the sandals. You say a couple things to him and it's a done deal."

"Dad has always had a way with young children." Cat smiled widely in a mix of pride and approval.

Chase sliced her a quick look. "It's the older ones that give me trouble."

Laredo chuckled and hooked a leg over one corner of the desk. "Tell me, Jake, have you started making a list of what you want Santa to bring you for Christmas?"

Brightening visibly at the change of topic, Jake turned to him. "Yeah, I gotta lot of things I'm putting on it."

"Like what?"

"I need chaps and a belt and a rope—"

"You already have a rope," Laredo reminded him.

The response was a quick wrinkling of the nose. "That rope's for babies. I need a gooder one."

"My mistake." Laredo struggled to hold back a smile.

"Do you think Santa would bring me a saddle? I sure could use one," Jake added with an adult like nod of emphasis.

"And you could use jeans, a winter coat, socks, and underwear," Sloan inserted. "He's outgrown just about everything he has."

"You have been shooting up like a little weed." Laredo gave the top of Jake's brown hair a playful ruffle.

Jake started to protest the mussing then suddenly remembered, blurting, "And an ATV of my own."

Laredo laughed outright. "Now there's a modern cowboy for you. Why walk when you can ride an ATV."

"Santa would bring me one, wouldn't he?" Jake sought confirmation from Chase.

Out of the corner of his eye, Chase caught the negative movement of Sloan's head. "Something tells me Santa will wait on a present like that until you're older."

"How old?" Jake wanted to know.

Chase shrugged. "You'll have to ask Santa that one."

Jake thought about that for a second and nodded, then gave Chase a bright look. "What do you want Santa to bring you for Christmas, Greypa?"

"Yes, tell us," Cat urged.

"I'm already getting what I want—all my grandchildren are coming home for Christmas."

Jake frowned. "That's not a present."

"Sometimes the best presents don't come all wrapped up in a pretty package," Chase told him.

Clearly not buying that, Jake switched his attention to Laredo. "What are you putting on your list?"

"I'm like your great-grandpa here," Laredo replied. "I've already got just about everything a man could want."

Chase ran a brief glance over the lanky cowboy, wondering if anyone else caught the small qualifying phrase Laredo had used. But with Jake in the room there was no time to mull over it as the young boy ran over to Jessy.

"You want a real present, don't you, Grandma?"

Jessy made a show of giving his question serious thought. "I would like a new bathrobe. Mine's getting a little old." But she could tell her grandson didn't think much of that as a gift. "And maybe a new set of spurs."

His face lit up. "I want some spurs, too."

"If your list gets any longer, Jake, Santa will think you're getting greedy." Sloan walked over to him and slipped off the crooked headdress. "Better let me have this before you get it dirty."

"And I'd better go start lunch." Cat half turned from the room, then paused to glance at Chase. "Did you want to lie down for a little bit before lunch?"

"No." His reply was quick and firm.

"You should you know," she countered.

The brief exchange swung Jake's attention to Cat.

"What do you want for Christmas, Aunt Cat?"

"I can tell you what she *needs,*" Chase declared before Cat had a chance to answer. "A husband."

"Dad." His name came out in a shocked breath.

"Well, it's the truth," he insisted. "If you had yourself a husband, you wouldn't be hovering around nagging me all the time."

"I don't nag." She bristled a little at the suggestion.

"Not much," Chase murmured.

All wide-eyed with wonder, Jake looked at her. "Can Santa bring you a husband?"

Cat threw her father an irritated see-what-you've-started look and forced a smile. "No, dear. Santa doesn't bring those kind of gifts."

"But if he can bring somebody a puppy, why can't he bring you a husband?" he reasoned.

"A husband is something a woman likes to pick out for herself," she explained with a great show of patience. "And, heaven knows, the pickings are very slim around here. Assuming I was looking, of course," she added, shooting Chase another searing look.

"Of course." Chase nodded, his expression softening. There was a wealth of understanding in his gaze.

Cat knew that he was fully aware of those moments of loneliness that crept up on a person after they had lost the one they love—not to mention all those unnamed longings that visited a person at nightfall.

"If you want, Aunt Cat, I can help you look for one," Jake volunteered.

One look at his earnest expression and Cat had no difficulty maintaining a smile. "I appreciate the offer, but I prefer to do the looking myself."

He cocked his head at a curious angle. "Where are you going to find one?"

His question had Cat firing an exasperated glance at Chase. Sloan saw it and came to her rescue, grasping her young son by the shoulders, his folded-up headdress tucked under her arm.

"Enough questions, Jake." She turned him toward the living room. "Let's go put your costume away."

"And then what?" He wanted to know even as she steered him in the direction of the wide oak staircase that led to the home's expansive second floor. "Can we go down to the barn and feed the horses?"

"We'll see." Sloan's murmured response drifted back to the den.

Laredo gave a wry shake of his head. "That boy can't slow down. If he's awake, he has to be moving."

"Trey was just like him at that age," Jessy recalled, then roused herself. "I need to get moving myself. It's time I checked on things at the ranch office."

When she stood, Laredo pushed away from the desk. "I'll tag along with you. I need to see if those parts for the generator were delivered. Catch you later." He flipped a casual wave in Chase's direction and followed Jessy out of the room.

As the pair swung toward the front door, Cat hesitated, then re-entered the den and set about collecting the coffee cups and placing them on the tray. Chase watched while she picked up the now heavier tray and balanced it on her forearm.

At the moment when she appeared ready to turn away from the desk, he said, "You mean you aren't going to bring up that business again about me lying down before lunch?"

"And be accused of nagging again? Not likely," she shot back.

"You do nag sometimes, Cat," Chase countered.

"If I do, it's only for your own good," she insisted, holding herself a little stiffly.

Pride. His daughter had always had an

23

abundance of that. But it was his awareness of her lightning quick temper that prompted Chase to overlook that proud and combative tilt of her chin. "I'm well aware of that, Cat," he assured. "But you need to recognize that while I may be old, I'm not an invalid."

"I know that." But there was a touch of sharpness in her voice.

"You have too much time on your hands and very little else to think about except me."

"Oh, please." Exasperation riddled her words. "You aren't going to start talking about a husband again, are you?"

"Why is that such a sore subject?" He leaned back in his chair in a show of relaxation to mask his close study of her reaction. "Are you absolutely against ever marrying again?"

"Of course not." Her response was emphatic and quick. "Why would I be when I've seen two perfect examples. First there was you and Hattie . . . Regardless of how much you loved my mother, I know your second marriage to Hattie was very fulfilling, but in a different kind of way. And anyone can see how happy Jessy is with Laredo." She paused, irritation flickering through her expression. "Although sometimes I get so mad at Laredo, I want to haul off and hit him!"

"Why?" Chase frowned in surprise.

"Because he obviously lets his pride stand in the way of going to that next step and actually marrying her. And why? Just because Jessy runs this ranch and he's only an ordinary cowboy. It's ridiculous."

"I don't think pride has anything to do with it, Cat."

"Then why doesn't he marry her?" she challenged.

"I suspect he has other reasons. Ones that don't bother Jessy, so they shouldn't bother us either."

Cat was quick to read between the lines, all her senses going on high alert. "Are you saying there's some truth to the rumors that Laredo is a wanted man?"

"I've never asked. And I never will." Unspoken was the order that she shouldn't either.

"Logan always liked him a lot," she recalled in an absent, musing fashion.

"Maybe you should think about taking a trip after the first of the year," Chase suggested in a deliberate change of subject.

A small, breathy laugh of surprise slipped from her. "Where did that come from? First you accuse me of turning into a nag, and now you're trying to get rid of me?"

Chase smiled at her half playful taunt. "That thought hadn't crossed my mind, but it is another good reason. Actually I was remembering that comment you made about the scarcity of eligible men around here. If you spend all your time here on the Triple C, you aren't likely to meet anybody. A change of scenery would be good for you anyway."

"And where would I go?" she countered, unimpressed by his suggestion.

"Go down to Texas. Spend a month or two with Quint and Dallas. It's been quite a while since you spent some time with your son and his family."

"Trade one ranch for another? I don't think so."

"Then fly over to England and stay with Laura. If it's a social life you want, she'll see that you get one. You know how full her calendar is all the time. I'm surprised she managed to work us in to come for Christmas this year."

Cat responded with a quick shake of her head. "The weather would be nasty at this time of year over there."

"Then go on a cruise somewhere warm," Chase argued, growing a little irritated by her quick dismissals.

"Alone? I don't think so." This time the shake of her head was firm and decisive. "Maybe I will fly back to Texas with Quint after Christmas. But if I do, it will be to spend some time with my new grandson, Josh." Cat smiled just thinking about the nearly two-year-old toddler and his head of red hair. "Face it, Dad—not everyone gets a second chance at love."

"And you damned sure won't if you sit around here waiting for it to come to you," he informed her.

This time she didn't rise to his baiting tone. "Enough, Dad. Why don't you come out to the kitchen and give me a hand with lunch? As you so succinctly put it—you're old, not an invalid."

"Don't get smart with me, girl," he warned but with a half smile. "This time you take care of lunch by yourself. I've got some thinking to do."

Catching the serious note in his voice, Cat eyed him curiously. "About what?"

"Guess you can blame Jake and all his talk about Christmas and presents." His gaze shifted to a front window as sunlight flared off the windshield of a pickup reversing away from the house. Jessy sat in the cab's passenger seat. "For one reason or another, it's been a good many years since all of us have been together for the holidays. It'd be good if I could come up with special gifts for each of you to mark the occasion."

"It would be," Cat agreed readily and turned to leave, adding over her shoulder, "Just give me your list once you have it done and I'll get them for you."

His response was a laugh-like snort. "Yeah, you'd like to know what your present's going to be. I know you. This year I'll do my own shopping, thank you."

Cat started to protest, then shook her head in amusement. "Whatever you say, but you're going to find out shopping isn't as easy as you seem to

27

think it is." She continued out of the den bound for the kitchen.

Chase could have told her that the difficulty usually depended on the object a person wanted to buy. But he wasn't about to arouse her curiosity any further, and wisely kept his silence while he pondered the possibilities. One was obvious; the rest weren't.

Chapter 2

By noonday, the chinook wind had diminished in strength to a stiff breeze. Most of the ranch yard's snow cover had melted; only the occasional shrunken drift lingered in the sheltered areas.

Crossing the ranch yard, Trey Calder angled toward the heavy-timbered bar. Christened Chase Benteen at birth he was the third Calder to bear that name. The distinction had early on earned him the nickname of Trey, and he'd answered to Trey ever since. The outdoor life of a rancher had left a bronze cast to the hard angles and planes of his face, features that were a hallmark of male Calders. He stood three inches over six foot in his stocking feet. The riding heels of his cowboy boots added another couple inches to that.

As he neared the barn, the side Dutch door swung open. Out hopped his young son who instantly clamped a hand on top of his cowboy hat to keep the wind from blowing it off. Trey allowed a small smile to play with the corners of his mouth at Jake's action then flicked a brief, identifying glance at Sloan when she appeared in the doorway behind their son.

By then Jake had spotted him. "Hi, Dad." He broke into a run, but the muddy ground sucked at his boots, giving a clumsy gait. "Wha'cha doing?"

"Looking for you."

"Guess you don't have to look anymore 'cause I'm here, huh?" Jake reasoned.

"That's right." Trey slipped an arm around Sloan when she joined them. "What have you two been up to?"

"I been working, Dad," Jake declared very matter-of-factly.

Fighting back a smile, Trey worked to match his young son's tone. "Get a lot done, did you?"

"Yup."

"Really." But the sideways glance he gave Sloan was skeptical.

"It's true," she assured him, with mock seriousness. "He helped feed the horses and gave Jobe a hand cleaning out the stalls, then held a horse for Tank while he trimmed its hooves."

"Tank said I was a real good helper." Jake fairly beamed with pride at the remembered praise.

"With all the work you've been doing, I'll bet you're hungry," Trey guessed.

"Real hungry," Jake confirmed with an emphatic nod. "Sure glad it's lunchtime. Mom and me was just headed to the house to eat. Mom said Aunt Cat would prolly have the food on the table by now."

"Let's hope so." By common consent, they all struck out for the Homestead, but at a pace that Jake's shorter legs could match.

"Hey, Mom." He turned, walking sideways.

"Do you s'pose Greypa has found a husband for Aunt Cat yet?"

"A husband?" Trey threw a puzzled frown at Sloan.

"Long story," she murmured in answer, then said to Jake, "I doubt it."

"Can I go ask him?" Jake asked with eagerness.

"May I," Sloan corrected automatically.

"But I want to ask him, Mom," Jake insisted, a determined set to his chin.

"No—I meant that you should have said 'May I' not 'Can I' go ask him." She found it hard not to let a small smile show.

"Well, can I?"

Sloan gave up the attempt to correct his grammar and waved a hand toward the house. "Go."

With permission granted, Jake took off at a run for the Homestead. She immediately called after him, "Don't you dare go in the house with those muddy boots on, Jake Calder! Take them off outside."

"Yes, Mom," he hollered back.

"So what's this long story about Gramps getting Cat a husband?" Trey asked now that Jake was out of earshot.

While she told him about the morning's incident, she kept an eye on their son just to make sure he remembered to remove his boots before he went inside.

But Jake clumped across the veranda's wooden floor straight to the bootjack near the front door, pried a foot out of first one muddy boot then the other, and launched himself at the door, throwing his weight against its heavy bulk to open it. Inside, he paused long enough to push it shut then struck out for the den. In his stocking feet, he had difficulty getting traction on the hallway's hardwood surface and reduced his headlong pace to a scampering trot.

When he reached the den's open doorway, he slid to make the turn into the room. "Hey, Greypa, did you find Aunt Cat a—husband?" He broke off the rest of his question and frowned in puzzlement when he saw his grandfather crouched behind the desk, only his head and shoulders visible. Jake moved to the side of the desk for a closer look. "Hey, Greypa, wha'cha doin?"

"Looking for something." Chase never glanced up from his search of the middle drawer's contents.

"Can I help? I'm a good looker, Greypa."

"No, I'll find it myself," he half growled the reply, shoved the middle drawer closed, pushed his chair back and lowered himself out of it onto one knee as he pulled open the bottom drawer. "The damned thing's gotta be here somewhere."

A protest formed, but he checked it when he heard the sound of the front door opening,

32

accompanied by his parents' familiar voices. He pushed away from the desk and ran back to the entry, arriving just as Cat joined him.

"That's good timing," Cat declared. "I was just on my way to let Dad know lunch is on the table. Jake, would you run and tell him?"

"Okay, but—" he hesitated, "but I think Greypa needs some help first."

"Why? Where is he?' Cat asked, the first glimmer of concern showing in her expression.

"On the floor behind the desk."

"On the floor? Oh, my God, he's fallen." Before she ever finished the sentence, Cat was running for the den, Trey and Sloan were only steps behind her. Not understanding what all the urgency was about, Jake brought up the rear.

Cat hurried behind the desk. "I'll help you up, Dad." Bending, she caught hold of his arm.

"Let go of me." He jerked it away and threw her a glare when she reached for him again. "What the hell are you doing?"

"I'm trying to help you," she snapped, then accused, "You had a dizzy spell, didn't you?"

"Like hell I did," Chase fired back, matching her explosion of temper.

"Oh, really." Cat jammed her hands on her hips, striking a challenging pose. "Then why are you on the floor?"

"Because I wanted to be. How the hell else am I supposed to look for anything in the bottom drawer." He made a half savage gesture at its contents.

Belatedly Cat noticed Jake, standing at the front of the desk, all eyes and ears. "Watch your language," she hissed at her father and jerked her head in Jake's direction.

"I wouldn't have any damned reason to be swearing if people would just put things back where they belong," Chase muttered and began pawing through the drawer.

"Just what are you trying to find?" Cat demanded, totally exasperated with him.

"My address book. The one that belongs in the top drawer." Straightening, he punched a finger at the proper location. "But it doesn't happen to be there."

"That's my fault, Gramps," Trey spoke up. "After I transferred all the names and numbers into the computer, I stuck the book over here in the cupboard."

As Trey moved to retrieve it, Chase demanded, "Why the hell did you do that?"

"What difference does it make why he did it?" Cat argued and swung away, stepping to the computer's keyboard behind the desk. "It was done. Now, whose number do you want? I can call it up faster than you can find it in that stupid book."

"If I wanted you to look up a number for me, I would have asked, now, wouldn't I?" Chase caught hold of the desk edge and used it to lever himself back into his chair.

"You're turning into such a grouchy old bear, Dad. I was simply trying to help you, and I get growled at for it."

"Maybe I shouldn't have done that," he conceded grudgingly. "But I got irritated. At my age, I don't have a lot of time to waste looking for stuff."

"Here you go, Gramps." With the address book retrieved from the cupboard, Trey placed it on the desk in front of him.

"Lunch is on the table. And if the soup's cold, it's your fault because you just had to have your address book." Plainly still angry with him, Cat pivoted sharply and stalked out of the den.

A faint sigh of regret slipped from him as Chase watched her go. He flicked a glance at Trey. "Something tells me I hurt her feelings."

"I think maybe you did." Trey smiled in commiseration, one of those man-to-man exchanges over the touchiness of women.

Before Sloan could speak up in defense of her sex, Jake chimed in, offering Chase some justification for his action. "But you only got mad 'cause Aunt Cat was fussing over you again. She needs a husband, huh, Greypa?"

"One would sure take the focus off me," he agreed absently and reached around for his cane. "We'd all better get in there for lunch or she'll never give me any peace."

"Are you gonna get her a husband?" Jake wondered, moving to Chase's side after he rose to his feet.

"Tell you what—let's both keep our eyes peeled for one," Chase suggested.

"Okay." Jake stood a little taller, proud that he had been asked to participate in the search.

"A word of warning, though"—Chase bent his head in Jake's direction, lowering his voice in a conspiratorial fashion—"don't say anything to Aunt Cat about it."

"How come?"

"Well, if she thought we had anything to do with finding her someone, she's liable to dig in her heels and refuse to have anything to do with him," Chase explained. "Women can be contrary that way. From now on we need to keep this husband thing between you and me. Deal?" Chase held out an open palm.

Jake readily gave it a slap of agreement. "Deal."

But to Sloan's ears, Chase's comments contained an undertone of chauvinism. "Tell me he isn't serious," she murmured to Trey.

"Partly," he admitted, amused by the whole scene. "But mostly he knows how to handle little boys. When I was his age, there was nothing more exciting than having a secret pact."

"I suppose," Sloan murmured, only half convinced.

"If you can think of a better way to stop Jake from talking about a husband for Cat—" He left it as an unfinished challenge.

"You made your point," she conceded.

In the dining room, each took their customary places at the table; Chase sat at the head of the table with Trey on his right and Sloan next to him while Cat occupied the chair at the foot of the table. The two chairs on Chase's left were empty but only momentarily as Jessy and Laredo made their tardy appearance in the room.

Chase offered the blessing after they were seated. Upon its conclusion, he raised his head and cast a sideways glance at the tawny-haired woman on his left. "Glad to see I wasn't the last to arrive. Cat informed me that if the soup was cold, it was going to be my fault." He removed the lid from the small, individual soup crock on his plate and inhaled the steam before sending a twinkling glance to Cat at the opposite end of the table. "The soup is not only hot, but it smells delicious."

"Heaping compliments on me will not get you on my good side." Her response had a definite cool edge to it.

Amusement was in the half chuckling breath he released. "You're getting more like your mother every day. Never could sweet talk my way around her either."

"I should hope not." Cat dipped a spoon into her soup.

Choosing not to bait her further, Chase directed his attention to the late arrivals. "So what kept you two? No problems, I hope."

"None. I was on the phone with Quint going over a few things at the Cee Bar." Jessy paused a beat. "That drought in Texas will drastically reduce the number of cattle he hoped to winter over. The graze just isn't enough and the pencil can't make the high cost of hay work."

"Quint knows that if he takes care of the land, the land will take care of him. It just might take a year or two," Chase stated, unconcerned by the news.

"He learned that from you," Jessy said in agreement then glanced at Cat. "By the way, he wanted me to tell you 'hi' for him, and to remind you that it isn't too late for you to fly down and spend Thanksgiving with them."

"I've thought about it," Cat admitted. "But it would be foolish to go there for just one day."

"Who said it had to be for one day?" Chase challenged.

"I'm sure you would like me to stay there longer so I wouldn't be here *nagging* you, wouldn't you?" The sweetness in her voice was all saccharine.

Chase raised one eyebrow, but chose not to reply. Before the silence could become awkward, Sloan filled the void. "Is there some reason you can't stay with Quint for a few days?"

"Not really. It's just that I know how busy he is right now. Quint has had very little free time since you bought the Slash R ranch from the Rutledge estate last year. As you well know, that more than tripled the size of your Texas holdings," Cat reminded her. "Quint has enough on his plate right now. And even though the Slash R adjoins the Cee Bar, access to it is difficult."

"I guess you can thank Tara for that—or blame her for it, depending on your viewpoint," Trey inserted, referring to his father's first wife. "Buying the Slash R was a good business move, but I doubt we would have bought it if Tara hadn't left the bulk of her estate to Laura and me."

"Even in death that woman managed to somehow involve herself in Calder affairs," Chase observed with a wry shake of his head.

"She did have a knack for that," Cat agreed, then idly recalled, "I can't say that I was surprised when I learned she had named you and Laura as the major beneficiaries. Almost from the day you were born, she looked at you two as the children she and Ty might have had if she hadn't walked out on him."

A harrumphing sound came from Chase's end of the table. "That marriage was on the rocks well before that," he declared.

During all this discussion about Tara, Jessy had taken no part in the conversation. Her silence on the subject was one Laredo was quick to note. He skimmed her profile with a sideways glance, trying to get a read on her. But Jessy had long ago schooled her features not to reveal her inner feelings, and now she excelled at it, a trait that any poker player would envy.

There had never been any doubt in Laredo's mind that Jessy had never liked Tara. But the other woman had always had an uncanny knack for insinuating herself into the lives of the Calder family. Wisely Tara had focused her attention on her ex-husband's children, fully aware that the rest of the family merely tolerated her presence. Laredo had long ago decided that Tara found some perverse form of pleasure in that.

The more he thought about it, the more convinced he became that Chase was right; Tara was doing it again; this time from the grave.

And that might be the very thing that was sticking in Jessy's throat at the moment.

Deciding a slight change of subject would be welcomed, Laredo provided the opening to Jessy. "This might be a good time to mention that suggestion Dallas made."

"What suggestion is that?" Trey wondered.

"Selling off the main ranch house at the Slash R along with the necessary acreage to encompass the helipad and access to the highway," Jessy replied. "I thought it was a very practical idea, considering that we've already decided we want to maintain our headquarters at the Cee Bar. The Slash R ranch house is much too lavish to be used as a foreman's quarters."

"Would you be comfortable with that decision?" Chase directed his question to Sloan; aware—as they all were—that Max Rutledge had been her childhood guardian.

"Absolutely," she replied without hesitation. "I have few good memories left of the place."

Trey exchanged a glance with his mother. "Looks like we can add one more thing to Quint's list of things to do."

"Which is one more reason I won't be going to Texas for Thanksgiving," Cat declared and proceeded to clear away the soup dishes while Jessy passed around the makings for sandwiches.

"Isn't anyone going to bring up the other elephant in the room?" Chase challenged.

"What elephant, Greypa?" Jake looked around the dining room with wide-eyed interest. "I don't see it. Where is it?"

"It's just a figure of speech, bud," Trey told him. "There isn't a real elephant in here." He smiled at Jake's obvious disappointment, then glanced at Chase. "I think Grandpa's talking about the summerhouse Tara built over in Wolf Meadow."

"Summerhouse." Chase snorted at the phrase. "If that's what you call it, then the Homestead is a log cabin. That place rivals anything Rutledge built at the Slash R, plus she added an airstrip. He just had a teensy little helipad."

"Trey and I were talking about it just the other day," Sloan began.

Chase pinned her with an arrow-sharp look. "Are you two thinking about moving over there to live?"

Catching his combative tone, Cat spoke up. "It would give them a lot more privacy than they have here."

"I'm not interested in *us* living there," Sloan said quickly. "But I am convinced you would have no trouble at all leasing the place as a summer retreat to various companies, or even individuals."

There was a full second of heavy silence at the table. When Chase spoke, it was in a carefully controlled but terse tone.

"The Triple C will not be turned into a dude ranch while I'm alive."

"Trey told me much the same thing," Sloan admitted. "Still, it seems such a waste for the place to sit unused, all locked up."

"She has a point," Cat agreed. "Someone needs to be living there. Otherwise it's just going to slowly deteriorate." The minute the words were out of her mouth, she pointed a warning finger at Chase. "And don't you dare suggest that I go live there!"

"I wouldn't waste my breath suggesting it."

"I should hope not."

"A decision of some sort has to be made about it. We can't keep putting it off," Chase stated, then glanced at Jessy. "When was the last time anyone checked on the place?"

"Fall roundup," she replied. "When we made our gather at Wolf Meadow, I rode over and took a look around. I didn't have a key so I couldn't go inside, but everything looked fine."

"Just the same, you might as well fly over there this afternoon and inspect the house inside and out, as well as all the outbuildings. See if it can be converted to an out-camp for that corner of the ranch."

"That would mean building a road to it, Gramps," Trey inserted, reminding Chase that the site was only accessible by air.

"That's a cost we'll have to weigh against its potential use," Chase replied.

"I have a meeting this afternoon, but I can fly over there in the morning," Jessy told him. "Would you want to ride along, Chase?"

He shook his head. "After riding an hour in that cramped cockpit, my arthritis would have me so stoved up, you'd have to pry me out of the plane. You and Laredo go. Why don't you ride along with them, Cat?" he suggested. "Do you good to get away for a bit. Have a change of scenery."

"You just want me out of the house so I won't be around to nag you," she retorted.

43

"That wasn't my reason at all," he stated, his exasperation showing.

"I'm sure it wasn't," Cat agreed. "But I can't go tomorrow anyway. I want to get a jumpstart on baking the pies for Thanksgiving, and get a few casseroles made ahead as well so all I'll have to do is pop them in the oven."

"Can I go with you, Grandma?" Jake piped up, eyeing Jessy with unabashed eagerness. "I like riding in planes."

"True. You've flown so often," Trey teased, but the observation sailed over Jake's head.

"I'd love to have you fly with me, as long as your mom says it's okay." Jessy smiled her answer.

"Mom won't care. Will you, Mom?" He turned an earnest look on Sloan.

"You can go, as long as you promise to be good." Sloan qualified her permission.

"I'm always good. Aren't I, Grandma?" he asserted with confidence.

"Almost always."

Through the rest of the meal Jake peppered her with questions. How high would they fly? Would they go through any clouds? How does a plane stay in the air? Could he take his gun along—a toy—so he could shoot any coyotes he saw? Why are some clouds gray and some white? Jessy tried to answer his questions truthfully, but she had to be quick to keep Laredo from offering one of his tall tale answers.

Finished with her own meal, Cat stood. "Anyone want dessert? There's some cake in the kitchen. Or fruit if you like?"

"Not me." Chase pushed his chair back from the table and reached for his cane. "I've got some phone calls to make. I'll be in the den if anyone wants me."

Cat watched him leave, then mused aloud, "I wonder who he's going to call?"

"Ask him," Laredo told her.

"I did. He wouldn't tell me, just went all mysterious and said it wasn't any of my business." An answer she clearly didn't like.

"Maybe it isn't," Laredo countered.

"More than likely he's calling some store to buy a Christmas present for one of us," Cat decided. "After the patrolman left this morning, Dad did talk about this being a special Christmas we'll be celebrating this year with the whole family getting together."

"I bet I know what he's gonna buy," Jake declared, then smugly pressed his lips tightly together rather than confess the secret he shared with his great-grandfather. He was a bit disappointed when no one took the bait and asked him what it was.

The single-engine Cessna Skylane swept through the wide blue sky while its shadow raced across the rough and broken land below it. Jessy was at

45

the controls, automatically scanning the country before her. Every low mesa and wide coulee had a distinctive characteristic that enabled Jessy to pinpoint her location in this vast emptiness. Laredo occupied the co-pilot's seat, his glance idly turning to look out the side window.

Buckled into his child's seat directly behind Jessy, Jake strained forward to tap the back of her seat. "Hey, Grandma. Are we there yet?"

"Almost," she answered with a slight turn of her head in his direction, then pointed to a spot slightly to the left of the airplane's nose. "Did you see that butte just ahead of us?"

Jake craned his head to the side. "The big one?"

"That's Antelope Butte." As always Jessy used any excursion with her grandson to teach him more about the Triple C. "The landing strip is just below it. Won't be long now."

Behind her, Jake settled back in his seat, content that his confinement wouldn't last much longer. Jessy pushed the plane's nose slightly below the horizon line to begin the descent.

Feeling the movement, Laredo looked back at Jake. "We're starting down, bud. Make sure your seatbelt's tight."

"Right." Obediently Jake gave it a tightening pull.

"I want to do a flyby to make sure the strip is in good shape," she said to Laredo. "Keep your eyes peeled for any buckling of the concrete."

"Will do."

Jessy made a low pass over the strip. Its lack of use in recent years was evident in the mix of tall grass and weeds that hugged the runway's edges. Some had taken root wherever there was a crack in the concrete surface. But the visual examination found no potentially hazardous break-up or heaving.

The plane landed without incident and taxied to the padlocked hangar. After nearly forty minutes of forced inactivity, Jake was all raw energy when Laredo swung him to the ground.

"Where are we gonna go first, Grandma?"

Drawing in a bracing breath, Jessy let her glance sweep over the stables and adjacent corrals to the left, the idle blades of windmill eleven, and the half hidden groundskeepers' quarters before coming to a halt on the low profile of the sprawling main house. It had been Tara's summer base, built on land she had purchased from the government, preventing Chase from gaining title to it until after her death. As always, the sight of it evoked memories—some bitter, but most just remembrances of the past.

"That first building," she told Jake, nodding in its direction.

"Bet I beat cha there," he challenged.

"I'll bet you do," Jessy agreed and watched him take off at a run. She and Laredo followed at their usual striding pace.

"It's been a good many years since I was here last," Laredo remarked. "Not that I ever came here all that often. Still, I forgot how well it blends into the butte's face."

Jessy studied the roof that was almost the same brownish color as the earth wall behind it. "It's one of the rare times Tara showed some restraint." A sudden smile flashed across her expression. "At least until you get to the inside."

As they crossed the driveway's paving stones to approach the house, Jake came running back to meet them. "I rang the bell, Grandma, but nobody came to open the door."

"That's because no one lives here." Continuing toward the front door, Jessy slipped the key from her jacket pocket.

"How come?" Jake persisted.

"To make little boys like you ask questions." Laredo reached down to give the front brim of Jake's cowboy hat a downward push over his eyes.

" 'Redo, don't." Jake frowned in displeasure and tipped it back up, but it served to distract him from that line of questioning. "Are we going inside, Grandma?"

"We sure are."

The prospect of exploring the unoccupied house clearly appealed to him, as evidenced by the way he sprinted back to the front door. With barely disguised impatience, Jake waited while Jessy unlocked it. He darted through the opening the instant she gave the door an inward push.

Everything inside was just as Tara had left it. But to Jake's disappointment, there was little to be seen. All the furnishings were shrouded in dust-protecting cloth, even the antlered chandelier that hung from the coffered ceiling. Jessy's inspection of the house amounted to little more than a cursory walk through of each room to check for any signs of a leaking roof or broken windows.

When they exited the last room and started down the wide hallway, Jake heaved a big, bored sigh and looked hopefully at Jessy.

"Are we done yet, Grandma?"

"All done." She smiled, as glad as he was that the task was complete.

With an uninhibited shout of "Yippee!" Jake ran ahead of them, the rapid clump of his booted feet echoing through the emptiness. He beat them to the front door, but was still struggling with its oversized handle when they joined him. Laredo opened it for him, then waited outside while Jessy re-locked it with the key.

"Chase pegged this place right when he called it a white elephant," Laredo remarked when Jessy turned, tucking the key back in her pocket. "What are you going to do with it?"

Jessy shook her head. "I wish I knew."

"Where to now, Grandma?" Jake stood poised at the edge of the weed-invaded stone walk.

"We're going to check the other buildings," she told him. "You can run on ahead."

Immediately he took off and Laredo fell in step with Jessy. "Let me rephrase my question," he said. "If you could do anything you liked, what would you want to do with it?"

"Anything?"

"Anything," Laredo confirmed.

"That's easy. I'd bulldoze it."

"Then do it. Auction off everything inside, give the proceeds to some charity, and tear the place down."

"You're serious." She eyed him with a mixture of hope and uncertainty.

"You're damned right I am. What else are you gonna do with a white elephant out in the middle of nowhere that you can't sell or give away?"

"True," she agreed, but he could tell she wasn't convinced.

"You're letting that practical streak get in the way," Laredo chided. "White elephants and practicality don't go together. If they did, someone in this family would have come up with a solution a couple years ago after all the paperwork came through giving the Triple C clear title to this place."

"You have a point," she conceded.

"Suggest it to Chase." Laredo smiled. "I'm betting he'll think it's a helluva good idea."

"I think I will." The minute the words were out,

Jessy felt that nameless tension easing from her. She headed toward the outbuildings with a new interest in assessing their potential use.

Laredo observed the subtle change in her mood, but wisely didn't voice it. Instead he kept Jake occupied, leaving Jessy free to look things over without any distractions.

When Jessy emerged from the caretaker's quarters, Laredo stood a short distance away watching Jake gallop his imaginary horse in a wide circle. His attention shifted to her as she approached him.

"Everything okay in there, too?"

She answered with an absent nod. "I'd forgotten the house had three bedrooms. We just might be able to use Wolf Meadow as an outcamp. Our manpower is spread a little thin in this sector. Usually it's not been much of a problem unless we have a hard winter."

"That would mean putting a connecting road in," Laredo reminded her.

"One of the old ranch roads used to come within three-quarters of a mile of old windmill eleven. Chase blocked it off and tore out the culvert when Tara gained title to Wolf Meadow. He wanted to make sure she couldn't use it." She cast a thoughtful glance in the direction of the old road. "It will take some work to make that road useable again, but it wouldn't be as costly as putting in a whole new road."

"It looks like you've come up with . . . at least a partial solution for this place," Laredo said.

Just as Jessy opened her mouth to reply, there came a shouted "Whoa!" from Jake. Both turned to look. Laredo smiled in amusement at the sight of the young boy veering off his wide circle into some taller grass.

"Looks like Jake has himself a pretend runaway." Laredo exchanged smiling glances with Jessy.

As always, Jessy used the opportunity to teach her grandson. "Let your horse run a bit," she called. "Don't pull back on the reins right away. He'll just fight you. Make him go in a circle instead. That will slow him down."

She watched in approval while Jake followed her instructions and brought his imaginary mount under control and started back toward them. Abruptly he stopped and stared at something to his left.

Jake pointed to it. "What's that little pen for, Grandma?"

There, half hidden by the tall grasses and weeds, were a series of fence posts that boxed in an area roughly ten feet square. Jessy stared at it for an uncomprehending second before she realized what it was.

"That's a cemetery plot, Jake," she told him.

"You mean like that place we got down by the river where Grandpa's . . . buried?" He frowned his uncertainty of the word's meaning.

"Just like that," Jessy confirmed. "Only this one's smaller. And badly neglected, too," she added in an undertone to Laredo, then walked over for a closer look, joined by both Laredo and Jake.

"Who's buried here?" Laredo tried to make out the name on the gravestone through the high weeds.

"Buck Haskell and his father," Jessy replied.

"Really." Laredo frowned in surprise. "I didn't remember that."

"Probably not. You probably hadn't been here on the Triple C much more than two or three years when Buck was killed in that head-on collision. We offered to have him buried in the ranch cemetery, but Vernon—Buck's dad—wouldn't hear of it. Of course, Vernon always blamed Chase for the way Buck turned out, insisting that if Chase hadn't testified against him, Buck would never have gone to prison that first time."

"Prison can bring out the worst in a person."

To Jessy's ears, Laredo's remark sounded like a statement of fact, as if from personal knowledge. She was reminded of how little she knew about his past. Just for a moment she was curious, but she quickly shut the door on the questions, leaving the past in the past, fully aware that knowledge of it wouldn't change anything.

"Have you noticed how quiet it's been?" Laredo asked.

"Peacefully so," Jessy agreed and let her glance wander over the isolated spot, hearing the soft

53

murmur of a breeze through the grass. "The quiet is something that always strikes me anytime I get away from the constant comings and goings at headquarters."

"That's true, but I wasn't referring to that kind of quiet," Laredo said.

Her sidelong glance was half amused and half puzzled. "Exactly what kind do you mean?"

His shoulders moved in a vague shrug. "It just seems we've had a long spell without anyone causing trouble."

"Is that a complaint—or merely an observation?" During these years they had been together, Jessy had learned to trust his instincts. It made her wonder if he was sensing something now, enough that she couldn't laugh off.

"Not sure what it is," Laredo admitted. "I just have this uneasy feeling I can't explain." With quicksilver swiftness, a lazy smile stripped the serious look from his face. "Probably nothing."

"Probably," Jessy agreed, aware that she felt a new need for alertness.

A slightly bored sigh came from Jake. "Okay, Grandma, where to next?"

"I think it might be time we flew home. What do you think?"

"Yes!" he cried with a fist pump for emphasis.

In the Homestead's kitchen, Cat gave the simmering cranberries a testing stir. Satisfied that they were thoroughly cooked, she picked up the sauce pan and started to pour them into a cut-glass serving bowl. With the first splash of the ruby-red fruit, the timer went off with a strident buzz.

"The pies must be done," she muttered, half in irritation.

"I'll take them out," Sloan volunteered and retrieved a pair of oven mitts from the counter.

"You are a jewel," Cat declared in appreciation. "Do you realize that once those pies are out of the oven, we're finished? The sauce is done, and all three casseroles are in the refrigerator, ready to be baked tomorrow. If you hadn't pitched in to help, I would still be at it this afternoon."

"The thanks go to Jessy for taking Jake with her." Sloan checked the centers of both pumpkin pies for doneness. "One of these might need another five minutes."

"That one pie tin was deeper than the other so I filled it fuller," Cat recalled and set the empty saucepan in the sink. Before she could carry the bowl of cranberries to the refrigerator, the telephone rang. Aware that Sloan was in the midst of transferring a hot pie to its cooling rack, Cat said, "My hands are free. I'll answer it." She picked up the kitchen's cordless extension. "Triple C ranch, the Calder residence."

"I'd like to speak to Chase Calder. Is he in?"

The voice on the other end was a warm baritone, very male and very compelling.

And not one Cat recognized, which only piqued her curiosity about its owner. "May I ask who's calling?"

"Wade Rogers."

The name wasn't one she was familiar with either. To her regret he didn't volunteer any further information. "Is this regarding business?" she guessed, certain a voice like that could sell anybody anything.

There was a definite hesitation before he answered. "It's personal," he replied evenly, effectively blocking any further questions.

"Just a moment, and I'll see if he's available."

"Thank you."

Keeping the telephone to her ear, Cat exited the kitchen and made her way to the den. Chase was behind the desk, rocked back in his chair and idly staring out the window.

She paused in the doorway. "You have a phone call, Dad. A Mr. Wade Rogers."

"Rogers?" he repeated with a slight frown.

"Yes. Wade Rogers. He said it was personal."

"Rogers." This time the name was said with recognition. "Of course." He rocked the chair forward and picked up the desk extension. "This is Chase Calder."

"Mr. Calder. This is Wade Rogers. I hope I'm not calling at a bad time."

"Not at all," Chase assured him and slid a glance at Cat, who remained in the doorway, the kitchen extension still held to her ear. "You can hang up the extension now, Cat. And close the doors when you leave."

Startled by that unexpected request, Cat was slow to react. When Chase continued to look at her—without resuming his conversation with Wade Rogers, she belatedly punched the button, breaking the connection on her phone, and moved to close the den's double doors.

Chase nodded his thanks and said into the phone, "I just spoke to your father the other day. I'm glad to say he sounded well."

As she drew the doors together, the front door opened and the silence in the house was shattered by Jake's voice shouting, "Mom! Mom, we're back! Where are you?"

Suddenly Chase's request no longer seemed so unusual to Cat as she guessed that he had probably seen Jessy drive up out front and knew Jake would come bursting into the Homestead, shouting the news of his arrival. And lately Chase sometimes had difficulty hearing if there was too much background noise.

With the doors closed, Cat crossed to the entry. "Your mother's in the kitchen," she told Jake as Jessy and Laredo walked in. "You're back early. I thought you'd be longer at Wolf Meadow."

"It didn't take as long as I thought either," Jessy

admitted and started across the hall. "Is Chase in the den?"

"Yes, but he's on the phone right now," Cat replied, then added, "Somebody called Wade Rogers. Does that name mean anything to you?"

"No, not really," Jessy said with a small shake of her head. "Why?"

"Just curious. I heard Dad telling him that he'd spoken to his father the other day, but I don't remember anyone named Rogers."

"Chase has dealt with so many people over the years that you can't expect to know them all. Some of them were bound to be before our time." Jessy shrugged it off as unimportant.

"True," Cat conceded and let the subject drop. Yet it wasn't as easy to block out the memory of that baritone voice. Its warm timbre lingered at the edge of her mind.

"Something smells delicious." Laredo sniffed the air. "You've been doing some baking while we were gone."

"A lot of it. And it's all for Thanksgiving. No sampling before," Cat warned.

"You do have coffee made, I hope," Laredo said, using the inflection of his voice to make it a question.

"Always. In fact"—Cat hesitated, a thought forming—"I think I'll see if Dad would like a cup. You two go help yourselves." As they headed for the kitchen, Cat retraced her steps to the den, rapped lightly on the door, then pushed it open and poked her head inside.

Chase looked up with a frown and cupped his hand over the phone's mouthpiece. "What is it?"

"Just checking to see if you'd like a cup of coffee."

"No, but I damned well would appreciate some privacy."

Stung by his abrupt response, Cat murmured a cool, "Fine." And closed the door, muttering under her breath, "You old bear."

Chapter 3

A platter of succulent turkey, roasted to perfection, made its way around the Thanksgiving table, with each spearing a thick slice for their plate—except for Jake, who claimed the drumstick. The yeasty aroma of freshly baked dinner rolls mingled with the sharp fragrance of sage dressing and the sweeter smell of candied sweet potatoes.

Soon every plate was crowded with helpings from the green bean casserole, mashed potatoes and gravy, and tart red cranberry sauce. Only Chase and Jake restricted their portions to a small sampling of everything.

Conversation during the first few bites centered around the food being consumed. Only after the edge was taken off their hunger did the table talk swing around to the usual topic of the ranch.

Trey began it. "I keep thinking about this idea of yours, Mom, to bulldoze Tara's place at Wolf Meadows—"

Before he could finish his comment, Chase interrupted. "I think it's the best damned suggestion for the place that I've heard."

"I don't disagree with it," Trey qualified. "But it's going to take some organization to accomplish."

"Only until the house is leveled," Chase reasoned.

"Then we're through with the place for good."

"True, but in the meantime, we'll need to contact various auction houses and decide which one we want to use. Naturally the contents will have to be itemized, maybe even photographed." He sent a quick glance at Sloan. "That's something you could handle."

"Be glad to," she agreed. "And I also have contacts at a couple auction houses. I could call them if you want."

"I, for one, would be grateful for any help you can give us," Jessy stated. "Ranching, I know. But this—well, it's out of my line."

"Which reminds me," Sloan said. "We'll need to choose a charity or charities that will benefit from the auction proceeds."

"That won't be all that hard," Trey said. "It's the logistics of the whole thing that I keep thinking about. You do realize everything in that house has to be crated up and hauled out of there, don't you?"

"You've just identified your first priority," Chase told him. "Putting in a road to it."

Trey answered with an agreeing nod. "We'll start on it tomorrow. I think we've got an old culvert at South Branch. I'll have it brought here to headquarters. Meanwhile Mike and I can put our heads together and figure out the best route to bridge that last mile."

"Once that road's in, one of the first things I

want you to do is dig up those graves. It's time Buck and his father came home," Chase stated.

His announcement brought a moment of silence to the table. Cat broke it. "Are you sure that's what you want, Dad?"

He answered by saying, "Ruth would want her boy beside her."

"Then that's what we'll do." Jessy ended any further discussion of that issue.

Chase made sure of it by changing the subject. "Have you talked to your mom about the toy drive for the Marines?"

"Talked to her?" Jessy echoed his question on a laughing note. "I went over there to tell her about it and, almost before I had the words out of my mouth, she was on the phone calling other ranch wives. By now, she's probably finalizing a list of toys to get and organizing a shopping trip."

"Speaking of Christmas," Cat began and split her glance between Jessy and Trey, "if you can spare a couple of the hands on Monday, I want to haul the decorations out of the attic and get started hanging the outside ones."

"No problem," Trey assured her.

"Unless it snows," Laredo inserted. "It's in the forecast for this weekend."

"As long as it isn't coming down on Monday, it won't be a problem," Cat told him. "In fact, it will add to the holiday atmosphere."

"That reminds me," Chase said. "Set an extra

place for lunch on Monday. The son of an old friend will be dropping by."

The phrase struck a familiar chord, sparking her immediate interest. "That son wouldn't be Wade Rogers, would it?"

Chase gave her a questioning look. "How did you know his name?"

"I answered the phone when he called and asked for you," Cat reminded him, struggling to sound matter-of-fact and conscious that she felt on the verge of blushing.

"Just the same, I'm surprised you remembered."

That voice wasn't one she was likely to forget, but Cat kept that bit of information to herself and asked instead, "Will he be staying long?"

"I doubt it. More than likely he'll leave early afternoon," Chase replied then cocked his head. "Why?"

"I merely wondered whether I need to make sure there was a room ready for him." She felt oddly disappointed that Wade Rogers's stay would be such a short one. Which was silly because she hadn't even met the man. For all she knew he could be fat and bald with hair growing out of his ears. Rather than dwell on that image, Cat pushed any further thoughts of Wade Rogers out of her head.

Come Monday morning seven inches of fresh snow covered the vast reaches of the Triple C ranch. No clouds remained, leaving the sun the sole occupant of the vivid blue sky. The air was brisk and the wind was still—a scene straight out of a Currier and Ives print. It was the ideal setting for holiday decorating—except for one thing.

Cat clamped gloved hands over her ears in a futile attempt to block out the deafening roar of the snowplow at work clearing the area in front of the Homestead. She wanted to scream at the driver to go somewhere else, then sighed in frustration, knowing she'd never make herself heard above the plow's diesel engine.

With teeth clenched, Cat lowered her hands and attacked the flaps of the cardboard storage box in front of her, one of several strewn across the pillared veranda, some empty and some waiting to be opened. Inside this particular box was a three-foot tall artificial tree, one of two that would occupy the decorative urns flanking the front door.

As she struggled to lift it out, first one flap then another got in her way. Try as she might, Cat couldn't muscle it out.

Just as she was about to give up and start over, a pair of gloved hands reached in and gave the tree the final tug, lifting it free of the box. At almost the same instant, a shrill whistle pierced the plow's loud din. Cat looked up and saw Laredo halfway up a stepladder holding a small wreath up to one of the front windows. He gestured to summon her.

Surrendering the tree to her helper, Cat pointed to the nearest urn, indicating it belonged there, then crossed to Laredo. With the snowplow's noise making conversation impossible, Laredo first held the wreath high on the window, then low, pantomiming his question of where it should hang. Cat responded in kind, using hand gestures until he had the wreath centered in the window.

After securing it in place, Laredo stepped off the ladder and tilted his head close to her, his glance flicking to a point beyond. "Who's the silver fox?"

Surprised that she could hear him, Cat first looked to confirm the snowplow was already some distance from the house and moving away; then Laredo's question registered. Suddenly she was conscious of an unfamiliar SUV visible in her side vision, but it was the tall gentleman standing at the front door who claimed her attention.

Everything about him screamed city—from his charcoal-colored topcoat and plaid muffler to his black-lace shoes, spattered with bits of snow. Not a hair on his bare head was out of place. And its color made Laredo's description "silver fox" singularly appropriate; it was a rich shade of pewter burnished with silver highlights.

"He must be Wade Rogers," she realized. "Dad said he would be coming by today."

Without waiting for a response, Cat hurried to greet their guest. When she reached him, he was about to knock on the door, an action that definitely marked him as a first-time visitor. Only strangers knocked; everybody else simply walked in.

"Mr. Rogers? You are Wade Rogers, aren't you?" Cat sought confirmation when he turned toward her.

"Yes, I am." The instant he spoke, his voice provided further proof of his identity.

One look at his strong, masculine features, the attractive grooves making a parenthesis of his mouth, and the compelling brightness of his dark, nearly black eyes, and Cat wanted to laugh that she had ever thought he might be bald and fat. This was a man as handsome as his voice.

"Welcome to the Triple C. I'm Chase's daughter, Cat Echohawk." She extended a hand to him.

"I believe we spoke on the phone."

"We did." She was secretly pleased that he recognized her voice even as she absorbed the sensation of his pleasantly firm handshake. The memory of it lingered after she released his hand and reached for the doorknob. "Please come in. I know my father is expecting you."

He stepped back, allowing her to precede him

into the house. Once inside, he paused on the rug and gave the bottom of his shoes a wipe on it. Cat first pulled off her gloves, then her stocking cap, and shoved them into the pockets of her parka before reaching up to fluff the ends of her hair, suddenly self-conscious about her appearance.

"Let me take your coat for you," she offered.

"Thanks." He shrugged out of the topcoat and passed both coat and scarf to Cat after tucking his gloves in a pocket. Underneath, he wore a dark sports jacket over an ivory-colored sweater. The bulk didn't at all detract from his trim build, Cat noticed.

"I imagine we'll find my father in the den," she told him and started in that direction. "I hope you had a good trip here," she added, feeling a need to fill the silence. "The roads weren't too nasty, were they?"

"For the most part, they were clear. I had no problems at all."

"I'm glad to hear it." As usual, the double doors to the den stood open. Cat walked in to find Chase seated behind the desk, as she expected. "Dad, Mr. Rogers has arrived."

"So I see." With some effort, he pushed out of his chair to stand upright with the aid of his cane.

Cat was pleased to see how quickly Wade Rogers moved to the side of the desk, without any appearance of haste, eliminating the need for the older man to come around to greet him.

"It's a pleasure to finally meet you face to face, Mr. Calder."

"Same here," he replied, shaking hands with him. "And the name's Chase to you. We don't stand on formality here at the Triple C."

"Chase it is," he said with a nod of understanding.

"Have a seat." Chase motioned to the chairs in front of the desk and shifted to resume his own seat. "Cat, bring us some coffee. You'd like a cup, wouldn't you, Wade?"

"Black. No cream. No sugar. If it isn't too much trouble," he added, directing a smiling glance at Cat.

"It's no trouble at all," she assured him. "We always have a pot brewed."

On her way to the kitchen, Cat paused in the entryway to hang up his coat and remove her own. As she lifted his coat onto the wall hook, she happened to glance at one of its sleeves. The texture and color of it brought another image flashing into her mind's eye. She turned with a start and stared toward the den, suddenly realizing that Wade Rogers had been the one who'd helped get the tree out of its box. A smile formed as she considered the thoughtfulness of the gesture, aware that he couldn't have possibly known who she was.

One more mark in his favor. She almost laughed aloud at the thought. Tallying up pluses and minuses on an attractive stranger—that was a schoolgirl's trait—and she was anything but a schoolgirl, or interested in a man's attention.

Yet even as the latter thought registered, Cat felt a little "And yet" sigh slip from her. Shaking it off, she hung up her parka and resumed her path to the kitchen.

Five minutes later she re-entered the den, carrying a tray with an insulated carafe of coffee and two cups. After she set it on the desk, she reached for the carafe, only to be stopped by Chase.

"Don't bother, Cat. We'll pour our own," he told her. "And would you mind closing the doors on your way out? Jake's bound to come barreling in soon and I don't want my chat with Wade interrupted."

"Of course." Cat smiled in understanding, splitting it between her father and the man in the wingbacked chair that faced the desk. As her glance lingered on him for a moment, she was quick to note the way Wade Rogers casually lounged in the chair, much as a frequent visitor would. "We're almost finished with the decorations outside. Then I'll be in to start lunch."

"Sounds like a teenager, accounting to me for her whereabouts, doesn't she?" Chase said to Wade, a twinkle in his eyes.

A little flustered and self-conscious, Cat was

quick to justify her comment. "I just wanted you to know where I'd be in case you needed something." With that she exited the room with as much dignity as possible.

As she paused to close the doors, she heard Wade remark, "That's the original map of the ranch on the wall back there, isn't it? My father described it to me many times."

Her father's reply was lost to her when the double doors clicked together.

The yeasty aroma of freshly baked rolls filled the kitchen when Cat opened the oven door to remove the pan. Little Jake appeared at her side almost instantly and shadowed her when she carried them over to the counter and the cooling rack that awaited them.

"They smell good, Aunt Cat," Jake declared with feeling. "Can I have one now? I'm hungry."

"May I," she countered, automatically correcting his grammar.

He gave her a puzzled look. "Don't you know if you can?"

It took an instant for his response to register. When it did, Cat laughed. "I think they're too hot right now."

As he sighed his regret, Sloan came up and rumpled his hair. "You don't need one anyway. It'll spoil your lunch."

"No, it won't. My tummy's real, real empty."

He pressed a hand against his stomach in emphasis.

"We'll eat as soon as your grandma and Laredo get here," Sloan promised and moved toward the oven. "Is the warming stone for the rolls still in here, Cat?"

"Upper rack," was the answer.

"And we gotta wait for Dad, too, I s'pose," Jake said with clear dismay as he lingered by the rolls, eyeing them with obvious longing.

"Your dad's not going to be here for lunch." Using an oven mitt, Sloan removed the stone and placed it in the bottom of the roll basket.

"How come?"

"He's at South Camp, helping haul hay out to the cattle. I imagine he and your other great-grandpa will have lunch together." Sloan laid a large, sturdy dishtowel over the warming stone and draped the ends over the basket's edge.

"And Grandma, too," Jake surmised.

"No, she won't be there," Sloan told him. "Don't you remember? You saw her with the other ladies at the commissary boxing up the toys." In an aside to Cat, she said, "They scored some incredible bargains shopping on black Friday."

"Good. That means all the money that was donated will spread further." Cat checked the large pot of beef and noodles and turned the burner to its lowest heat setting.

Boredom claimed Jake. With typical abruptness, he turned away from the tantalizing rolls and broke for the doorway to the dining room.

"Where do you think you're going, Jake?" Sloan demanded, a mother's natural suspicion surfacing.

Brought up short, Jake swung back in exasperation. "To see if Greypa opened the door yet?"

"Don't you worry about that door. Just stay here with us," Sloan ordered.

"But, Mom," he protested with great drama. "I want to tell Greypa about the snow fort me an' Luke an' Danny built."

"Luke, Danny, and I built," Cat corrected without thinking.

"You weren't there, Aunt Cat," Jake declared.

Before Cat could explain about his misuse of pronouns, Sloan inserted, "There will be plenty of time for you to tell Greypa about your fort at lunch."

He opened his mouth to argue the point, then correctly interpreted his mother's stern-eyed look of warning that this point wasn't open to debate. So he settled for simply asking, "How long before lunch?"

"Everything's ready. We can start dishing up as soon as your grandma and Laredo get here." Quick to see the next question forming in Jake's eyes, Sloan added, "And—no, I don't know how long that will be."

With a great show of reluctance, he dragged himself back to the kitchen table and, more or less, flung himself onto one of the chairs. Disgruntled and out of sorts, he demanded, "How come Greypa's got the doors shut anyway?"

"So he could visit with his friend in private."

"But Greypa'd want to see me if he knew I was here," Jake reasoned.

Sloan just smiled. "Nice try."

The corners of his mouth turned down in defeat as he slumped even lower in the chair. From the entryway came the sound of the front door opening, footsteps entering, and a man's muted voice. Jake immediately brightened.

"That's 'Redo."

Cat smiled her amusement with his reaction. "So it is. I tell you what—why don't you go knock on Greypa's door and tell him lunch is ready."

"Oh, boy." He was off the chair in a flash and racing out of the kitchen.

"Just knock," Sloan called after him. "Don't open the door."

"'Kay, Mom." His answer floated back from the dining room.

"That boy," Sloan murmured, but with obvious and genuine affection as Jessy and Laredo made their way into the kitchen.

"I swear Jake only has two speeds. Stop and go," Laredo declared, rubbing his hands together to warm them.

"Trey was just like that at his age," Jessy recalled, then made an assessing sweep of the lunch preparations in progress. "Need some help?"

"Everything's ready. Just needs to be dished up," Cat replied.

With so many hands to help, the task was accomplished in short order, leaving only Cat in the kitchen. She cast a glance around the counter and stove top to make sure nothing had been forgotten, then caught a glimpse of her own reflection in the oven door's glass front. She bent down slightly to check her appearance, touching fingers to her dark hair.

Lips curving in amusement, she sent a glance heavenward. "I'll bet you're up there smiling at me, Logan, for being so female I want that handsome Wade Rogers to think I look attractive." She turned a little serious. "It's good to feel this alive again, though. You don't mind, do you?" The minute the soft question slipped from her, an easy peace settled over her. "Of course, you don't."

She entered the dining room at the same moment that Wade Rogers strolled in alongside the much slower moving Chase. There was instant eye contact between them, and it was a heady thing. They exchanged small nods of greeting.

The moment Chase paused in the doorway, Jake was at his side. "Greypa, I've been waitin' an' waitin' for you to come out. Me an' Danny an' Luke built us a snow fort. Aunt Cat thinks she helped 'em, but it was me. And—"

"Whoa there, son." Chase held up a shushing hand. "You need to remember your manners. The first thing you do is greet our guest. Wade, this whirlwind is my great-grandson, Jake Calder. Jake, meet Mr. Rogers."

With shoulders squared and his expression solemn, if a little impatient, Jake thrust out a hand. "How do you do, sir?"

Adopting Jake's man-to-man attitude, Wade bent slightly to shake his hand. "How do you do, sir. I'll be interested to hear about that snow fort of yours later."

Jake's eyes got big with excitement. "Really?"

"Really," Wade assured him.

"He said later," Chase reminded him and continued with the introductions, skipping over Cat with a simple—"Of course you've already met my daughter"—and finishing with Laredo. "Last, but far from least, Laredo Smith, who's a member of the family in all but name."

"A pleasure," Wade said as he gripped Laredo's hand. "Laredo. That's an unusual name."

"Definitely colorful," Laredo agreed. "I guess

some parents do that when they've got a last name as common as Smith."

"Good point," Wade conceded, matching Laredo's easy smile.

Jessy smiled to herself at the deft way Laredo had deflected the comment without revealing anything. He was a master at it, just like that air of friendliness he projected, all the while sizing the man up, assessing and weighing everything from the nuances of his speech pattern to his body language. All the ranch hands were convinced Laredo simply had a nose for trouble. If he did, Jessy believed it was based in his ability to read people.

Privately Jessy was curious to know what conclusion Laredo had drawn about their guest as everyone took their seats around the table. Her own first impression was favorable, but as always she reserved judgment until she heard Laredo's opinion, having learned over the years to trust his instincts.

After the blessing was given, the serving dishes were passed around the table, and any talk was mainly centered on the food. As everyone dug into their meal, there was a momentary lull in the conversation.

Cat filled it. "Dad told us that this is your first visit to the Triple C."

"That's right, although my father has talked about it so much that it all seems very familiar to me." Wade paused a beat and smiled a moment to himself. "After I turned off that highway and drove through the gate, then drove and drove the forty miles to here, I got a clear understanding of what Father was talking about when he said, 'It takes a big chunk of ground to fit under a Calder sky.'"

"How true," Sloan agreed. "The first time Trey brought me here, I felt a little bit like that. It doesn't matter how much you hear or read about the Triple C, you don't really grasp any of it until you're actually here."

"What part of the country do you hail from, Mr. Rogers?" Laredo asked, and Jessy guessed immediately that Laredo couldn't place the man's accent.

"Here, there, and everywhere," he replied. "I was born while Father served in Congress. After college, I went to work for the State Department and ended up being posted in half a dozen or more countries around the world."

"That has to be an interesting career," Sloan stated.

"It's like most jobs that sound very glamorous— but the reality is usually something else."

"Are you stationed here in the States now?" Cat wondered.

After a slight hesitation, he replied, "In a manner of speaking. You see, I resigned from the State Department a few years back. Now I work as a private consultant, usually for companies with overseas business interests."

"So what brings you to Montana?" Laredo eyed him curiously while he dipped his knife into the butter for his roll.

"I had some business in the general area, and since I had a couple free days on my calendar, I decided to trade on my father's friendship with Chase and wrangle myself an invite. After hearing so many stories about the Triple C, the thought of being so close and not seeing it for myself—well, I just didn't want to pass up the chance," he concluded.

"We're glad you didn't," Cat said with a wide smile.

"So am I," Wade replied, returning her smile and holding her glance long enough that Jessy noted it. She shot a look at Cat, and caught that tell-tale glow about her face. She gave Laredo a little nudge and tipped her head in Cat's direction. Like her, he observed the very personal interest she was taking in their guest. And his reaction was to make a closer study of Wade Rogers.

"So where do you live now?" Cat asked, with seemingly polite curiosity.

"In one of the D.C. suburbs, on the Maryland side."

"Maybe you should ask him next whether he's married, Cat," Chase suggested, his head cocked in her direction.

"Dad—" She uttered his name in a breathless protest and shot a self-conscious and embarrassed glance at Wade. He avoided eye contact, directing his attention to the food on his plate. Yet Jessy was almost sure he was fighting back a smile.

"Well, the way you've been bombarding him with questions," Chase began in defense of his comment, "I thought you might be checking him to see if he was good husband material."

"Dad." Cat glared at him to shut up.

Before Chase could respond, Wade spoke. "As it happens, I'm a widower. I lost my wife to cancer a few years back." Nothing in his expression or tone of voice revealed any awareness that this topic might be awkward.

Unnoticed, Jake slipped off his chair and trotted around to Chase's side, laying a hand on his arm to claim his attention. "Greypa, is he the guy you're going to get Aunt Cat to be her new husband? You know, for Christmas."

At the same moment that Chase tapped a silencing finger against Jake's mouth as if to remind him it was their secret, Sloan blurted an embarrassed, "Jake, you shouldn't ask questions like that. You get back here on this chair right now," she insisted and threw an apologetic glance at Cat.

Cat was too furious to speak, certain she had never been so totally humiliated in her life. In her youth, she would have thrown her napkin on the table and stormed from the room. Now she sat in stiff silence and poked at her food, seething inwardly.

"I don't know what you must think of this family, Mr. Rogers," Sloan began, speaking to cover Cat's silence. "My son—"

Chase interrupted, smiling at Wade, a knowing gleam in his eyes. "What she's trying to explain is it's one of those private family wars I'm having with my daughter. And young Jake here is a good needler." He patted the boy's shoulder and nudged him toward his chair.

"Obviously it's an inside joke that's best ignored." Wade directed his reply to Chase, but made a point to include Cat by way of a reassuring side glance.

Only slightly mollified, Cat murmured, "You're understanding is appreciated." Try as she might, she couldn't keep the stiffness out of her voice— or shrug the whole thing off as easily as he seemed to be doing.

"Say, Jake," Chase inserted as the boy climbed on his chair, "you never did tell me about that snow fort you built."

"It's a good 'un, Greypa," Jake declared and immediately launched into a full description of it, who worked on it, and what each one did.

When others joined in with comments and questions, Cat was never so glad to have such a nonsensical topic dominate the conversation.

Along the way, she did her part to keep it going, determined to have it carry them through the rest of the meal, if possible.

"Sounds like quite a fort," Wade remarked.

"Want'a see it?" Jake sat forward, all eagerness. "I'll show it to you after we're through eating."

"Maybe another time," Wade replied, then let his glance encompass all at the table. "I know it's not polite to eat and run, but I'll have to be leaving right after lunch if I plan on making my flight."

"But it won't take long," Jake began in protest.

Sloan placed a silencing hand on his arm. "I think you forgot that you're going sledding with Luke and Dan this afternoon."

"Oh, yeah." Jake pressed his lips together in deep thought, then glanced at Wade. "I'll show you another time."

"Sounds good," Wade agreed, smiling.

Cat remained silent, struggling with an odd mixture of disappointment and relief that Wade would be leaving so soon. "Maybe another time." That's what he'd told Jake. She suspected that he had been deliberately vague because he knew there wasn't likely going to be another time. She knew she regretted that and carefully didn't examine the reason for it too closely.

At lunch's conclusion, Wade lingered over one cup of coffee, then pushed back from the table. "As much as I would like to stay, it's time I took my leave of everyone." Rising, he extended a hand to Chase, negating the need for him to stand. "It was good to meet you at last."

"The pleasure was all mine." Chase briefly gripped Wade's hand, holding his gaze. "Stay in touch."

"Will do." Wade nodded, but Cat sensed it was more a perfunctory response than a commitment.

As he began his good-byes to the others, Cat saw her opening and rose from her chair. "I'll get your coat for you."

By the time she retrieved his coat from the wall hook, Wade joined her in the entryway. Conscious of the flutterings in the pit of her stomach, Cat waited while he shrugged into his coat and mentally rehearsed the things she wanted to say, barely registering his compliments on the noon meal.

"I'm glad you enjoyed it," she answered automatically and started to launch into her speech. "Mr. Rogers—"

"I thought we agreed that it was just Wade, not Mr. Rogers." He smiled, the action carving those attractive male dimples in his cheeks again.

She was momentarily distracted—and a little thrown—by the sight of them. "Wade," she corrected herself, conscious of the slight quaver in her voice. "I want to apologize for all that talk at lunch today about a husband. I know it had to feel a bit awkward."

He tipped his head at a thoughtful angle. "I suspect it was more awkward for you than me."

Ignoring his observation, Cat continued, "Anyway, I want you to know—"

"—that you're not interested in me in that way," he finished for her.

She hadn't planned to put it quite that bluntly. "Something like that, yes," she admitted, feeling even more uncomfortable.

"Even though I guessed that—actually hearing you admit it—suddenly I'm sorry you feel that way." At his slightly reluctant admission, Cat found herself at a rare loss for words. As if sensing it, he offered his hand in farewell. "Let me thank you again for your hospitality."

"Anytime." Cat struggled to get the word out, her pulse skittering madly at the brief touch of his hand.

He held her gaze a second longer then turned away. Cold air rushed into the entry when he opened the door. It swirled around Cat even after Wade closed the door behind him. The click of the latch snapping into place broke the restraint she had placed on herself.

Hands clenched, Cat swung away from the door. "Why? Why? Why?" she berated herself in a barely audible murmur.

"Why did I react like that?"

Yet the reason was obvious, even to Cat. Pride. She had such an abundance of it. And in her determination to convince him she wasn't some man-hungry widow, she had been trapped by her own pride, totally incapable of responding in kind when Wade had indicated an interest in her. Cat knew she was attracted to him, sufficiently so that she was curious to know where it might lead.

"Anytime." The word echoed in her mind, with all its undertones of polite indifference, and total lack of encouragement for Wade to come back.

She told herself it was probably for the best that this had happened. Otherwise she would have lived in hope that he would come back to the ranch. At least now she knew that would never happen. The best thing was to block him from her mind, forget she'd ever met someone named Wade Rogers.

With a determined lift of her head, she retraced her steps to the dining room, entering just as Laredo emptied the contents of the carafe into his coffee cup. Cat immediately seized the excuse to gain a few more moments to herself.

"Here. Let me take that and I'll fill it back up." She reached for the insulated carafe before Laredo could set it back on the table.

"Don't need to fill it for me," Chase stated. "I've had enough."

"There are others who might want a cup," Cat reminded him and headed for the kitchen.

Chase watched her leave, then slid a wry look at

Laredo. "I get the feeling she hasn't forgiven me for teasing her about Wade," he said, without an ounce of remorse in his voice.

"And I have the feeling you're hoping she gets so mad that she'll stop talking to you at all," Laredo replied with a knowing look.

"Put a quick end to the nagging, wouldn't it?" Chase countered, eyes twinkling, then pulled in a deep breath and released it in a satisfied sigh. "It's been a full morning . . . and a busy one. Think I might stretch out and close my eyes for a bit." He retrieved the cane propped against the arm of his chair, and dipped his head toward the kitchen. "If she wonders where I am, let her know I'll be in my room."

Jake stared at him in amazement. "Are you really going to take a nap, Greypa?"

"Yes, Jake, I really am." Chase pushed out of his chair and headed for the west wing, the end of his cane thumping the floor with each stride.

Worried, Jake risked a sideways glance at his mother. "I don't have to take a nap before I go sledding, do I? 'Cause Luke—he's 'specting me right after lunch."

"If you finish your milk, you can skip the nap."

Jake didn't give her a chance to reconsider, grabbing the milk glass and downing its contents in two long gulps. "All done," he announced, pushing the glass on the table and sliding off his chair in one continuous motion. "Let's go."

With an amused shake of her head, Sloan stood up and tossed a glance at Jessy. "I guess I didn't really want that second cup of coffee."

"Good thing." Jessy smiled back at her. The small smile stayed in place while she listened to the run of conversation between Sloan and Jake when she joined him in the entry. Jake was still chattering away when they went out the front door. The silence was instant. "It's amazing how quiet the house seems after Jake leaves," she remarked to Laredo.

His only response was an agreeing sound as he continued to contemplate the dark surface of his coffee. Jessy made a sideways study of him, noting the expression of deep thought.

Curious, she asked, "What's those wheels of yours turning?"

It was a moment before he answered. "That Rogers guy." He raised his cup to his mouth and took a long sip from it.

"What about him?"

His shoulders shifted in an idle shrug. "Out of the blue, this guy calls Chase and invites himself here. Claims he wanted to see the ranch."

"What's so unusual about that?"

"Nothing," Laredo agreed, then met her glance. "It's funny though, the whole time he was here, he never budged from the house."

"How could he with all the snow we have?"

He dismissed that excuse with a quick shake of

his head. "No. Something tells me he had another reason for coming here."

"You don't really think he wants to cause us trouble," Jessy said with open skepticism.

"Even you have to admit something doesn't smell right."

"Not to your nose," she countered.

"Have it your way." As usual, Laredo didn't argue and simply pushed his chair back from the table. "But I'll take odds that we haven't seen the last of him."

Jessy stood up. "I think you're forgetting that he's the son of a long-time family friend."

"That's what Chase said, too." But he remained unswayed by the fact.

She started to remind him that Chase wouldn't lie, then caught back the words. It was Laredo's nature to be suspicious of anyone he didn't personally know. His instincts were usually right, but this was one case where time would prove him wrong. Jessy was sure of it.

Chapter 4

Moonlight glistened on the snow pack that edged the ranch yard and turned the exposed and rutted ground a deep black. Bundled against the night's chill, Sloan emerged from the Homestead and crossed to the steps. There, she paused to scan the yard for any movement that might indicate Trey was on his way back.

All was still. She focused her attention on the old barn and the light that showed in one of its small windows. Down the steps she went and struck out for the old heavy timbered barn. The cold air nipped at her skin and turned each exhalation of breath into a steamy vapor. Automatically Sloan quickened her steps to reach the barn's promised warmth.

The temperature inside the barn was a good ten degrees warmer. Sloan noticed the change the instant she stepped inside. At almost the same instant she spotted Trey's familiar tall frame as he stepped out of a stall halfway down the wide alleyway.

"Hey, there," she called out softly when he swung back to close the door behind him.

His head turned her way, the brim of his hat shadowing his eyes, but his smile of welcome was clear to see. "This is a nice surprise."

"I thought it might be." She crossed to his side

and let his encircling arm draw her against him. "Jessy said you'd come down here to check on an injured horse."

Her side-glance took note of the stall's occupant, a yearling filly currently nosing at the hay in its manger. The thickness of the animal's winter coat dulled its sorrel color and almost hid the scattering of cuts along its withers and hips.

"What happened to her?" Sloan asked.

"Somehow she broke through the ice down at the river," Trey replied. "When the boys took hay out this morning, they found her, soaking wet and blood oozing from a half dozen cuts."

"But how did she get cut up like that?" Sloan frowned.

"Ice can be as sharp as a razor. But she has one nasty gash that's a little too deep and ragged to be from ice," he explained. "If I had to guess I'd say she probably got it from a submerged tree limb. She'll be fine. So, have you got Jake all tucked in for the night?"

"All tucked in, and he's sound asleep. I thought about going through the photos I took at Wolf Meadow yesterday to start compiling an inventory list, then I decided to come find you instead." She snuggled closer to him, relishing the warmth of his body heat.

"Cold?" he guessed.

"Frozen," Sloan admitted. "I don't think I'll ever get used to your Montana winters."

"Miss those warm Hawaiian breezes, do you?"

"A little."

"Maybe we can slip away for a week or so in January and introduce Jake to the Pacific Ocean."

"Is that a promise?" Sloan tipped her head back to look at him. "Before you answer, be warned that I'll hold you to it if you say 'yes.'"

"In that case"—Trey arched an eyebrow, eyes twinkling—"maybe I'd better say that it's a definite 'maybe.'"

"Not fair." She emphasized her reply with a playful poke in the ribs, his wool-lined parka absorbing much of the poke.

He turned serious as he ran a searching look over her face. "You are happy here, aren't you?"

"Happier than I've ever been in my whole life," she assured him, "even if I never set foot in Hawaii again."

"Just wanted to be sure." He made his tone deliberately light, as if his question hadn't been a serious one at all. "Ready to head up to the house?"

"If you're done here?"

"I am." Keeping an arm around her shoulders, he guided her toward the door.

Outside the barn, Sloan waited while he turned off its interior lights and closed the door behind him, checking to make sure it was securely latched. Side by side, they struck out for the Homestead.

Sloan lifted her gaze to the large, two-story structure, its white brick revealed as a pale color in the moonlight. Red, blue, and green lights twinkled around the twin trees flanking the front door as well as the wreaths hung in each front window.

"The house looks so beautiful all decked out for Christmas," she murmured, unconsciously giving voice to her thoughts.

The sight of it triggered another thought in Trey's mind. "In another couple weeks it'll be time to decorate the barn for our annual Christmas party."

"It's always the last Saturday before Christmas, isn't it," Sloan recalled. "That sounds far away, but it really isn't, even though Thanksgiving was only a week ago. Which reminds me, I'll be gone most of tomorrow."

"Where?" It was an idle question, born of casual curiosity.

"A couple of us ranch wives are going to Miles City to buy toys for the Marines' campaign. We have our list done, so hopefully it won't take long once we hit the stores."

"I like the way you said that." His mouth curved in a pleased smile.

"Said what?" She slid him a puzzled glance.

"Us ranch wives. It tells me you finally feel like one of them."

Sloan thought about it and nodded. "I guess I do."

"See the stars." The gloved hand resting on her shoulder lifted, a finger pointing skyward. "On cold nights like this they always remind me of ice crystals scattered across a black sky."

Scanning nature's stardusted canopy, Sloan nodded in agreement, murmuring, "They're beautiful."

"Almost as beautiful as you are."

Surprised by the compliment that seemed to come out of nowhere, she turned her head to look at him. "I do believe you're putting the make on me."

"And what's wrong with an old married man putting the make on his wife?" Trey countered with a challenging lift of an eyebrow.

"Nothing at all." Her upturned face invited his kiss, and Trey was quick to oblige, his head dipping down, his mouth covering her night-cooled lips, heating them both.

When they parted, their eyes locked for a long moment, but neither spoke. All that needed to be said was communicated with that look. An easy silence ran between them as they resumed their path to the Homestead.

Sloan broke it when they reached the columned front porch. "Do you know what would be good now?"

"Something tells me it's not going to be what I'm thinking," Trey guessed.

"A hot cup of cocoa."

"Nope, that isn't what I had in mind."

Well aware of that, Sloan laughed, and Trey responded with a wide smile of his own. "My turn will come later."

"You sound awfully confident of that," Sloan teased as they entered the house.

"Damn straight I am 'cause I know you love me." He shrugged out of his sheepskin-lined parka and draped it on a wall hook.

"And you love me," Sloan countered, unbuttoning her own parka. "Which is why you're going to help me fix that cocoa."

"I think that's called wifely blackmail," Trey chided with affection, then flicked a glance toward the living room where the sound of the television could be heard. "First we'd better see if anyone else would like some cocoa."

But when they crossed to the living room, Trey was surprised to find his mother was the room's sole occupant. "Where is everybody?"

Jessy pulled her attention away from the program she was watching. "I'm not sure but I think Cat's in the kitchen, and Laredo left shortly after you went to the barn."

"So early?" Trey said with some surprise.

"He claimed he wanted to figure out where to install the hot tub I'm getting him for Christmas," she replied with a disbelieving smile.

"You're getting a hot tub to put at the Boar's Nest?" Trey grinned at the thought.

"According to Laredo, I am."

For the life of him, Trey couldn't imagine his mother lounging in a hot tub, but if anyone could coax her into one, it was Laredo. "Gramps called it a night, did he?"

"No, he's in the den. Wade Rogers phoned and he took the call in there where the television wouldn't bother him."

"That name sounds familiar." Trey frowned, trying to recall where he'd heard it. "I can't place it, though."

It was Sloan who answered. "He's the son of someone Chase knows—the one who stopped by on Monday when you were at South Camp."

"You mean the one Jake decided was going to be Cat's new husband." His smile widened into a grin as he made the connection to Wade Rogers.

"That's the one." Sloan nodded, then directed her attention to Jessy. "We're going to make some cocoa. Would you like a cup?"

"I'll pass."

Sloan glanced at the closed doors to the den. "Should we check with Chase?"

Jessy waved aside the question. "Just make him a cup. If it's fixed, he'll drink it."

"Will do." He tucked a steering hand under Sloan's arm and turned her toward the kitchen. "Come on, little miss cocoa maker, let's get this show on the road."

Jessy had been right when she guessed that Cat

was in the kitchen. She was standing at the counter, pouring a dark liquid into an over-sized plastic bag containing a large roast. She spared the pair a glance when they walked in.

"How's the filly?" she asked Trey.

"She'll be fine. What's that you're fixing?" He bobbed his head, indicating the plastic bag.

"I ran across a new marinade recipe that I decided I wanted to try on tomorrow's roast. It recommends letting it set overnight." Cat zipped the bag shut. "So what are you two up to?"

"Sloan decided she wanted some hot cocoa." Trey removed the jug of milk from the refrigerator and held the door open for Cat while she placed the pan with the marinating roast in its bag on a cleared shelf. "So far we have orders for three cups. Care to make it four?"

"Isn't Dad having one?" She glanced at him in surprise.

"That's who the third one's for, although he doesn't know it yet." He let the door swing closed and handed the milk jug to Sloan.

"Didn't you ask him?" Cat glanced his way with a questioning frown.

"Couldn't. He was on the phone." Trey paused a beat, a teasing light suddenly dancing in his eyes. "Actually he was talking to your future husband—at least, according to Jake."

"My—" Cat broke off that phrase. "He was on the phone with Wade Rogers."

95

"That's the man," he confirmed.

Was this a second chance? The question held Cat motionless for an instant. She honestly didn't know whether it was or not. But she realized she would never find out if she didn't take advantage of this opportunity. Ignoring the odd tingling sensation she felt, Cat moved toward the living room.

"Hey, you never said whether you wanted some cocoa," Trey called after her.

"No, thanks." The way her stomach was churning, she doubted she could keep it down.

When she walked into the living room, two things registered at once—the sight of Jessy sitting alone on the couch and the closed doors to the den. Immediately Cat altered her course and crossed to the latter.

She knocked once on the door and pushed it open. As she expected, Chase was seated behind the desk, the telephone to his ear. Irritation flickered in his expression as his gaze touched her.

"Just a minute," he said into the mouthpiece, then cupped a hand over it. "Did you need something, Cat?"

Fighting back an almost paralyzing attack of nerves, Cat plunged ahead. "Trey said you were on the phone with Wade Rogers. I'd like to speak to him when you finish."

He showed his surprise at the request with the lift of an eyebrow and a long, considering look.

Without responding directly to Cat, he removed his hand from the receiver's mouthpiece and said into it, "Before I let you go, Wade, my daughter wants to speak to you. Hang on." He held out the phone to her.

For a moment her legs felt like jelly. Somehow Cat managed to cross to the desk and take the phone from him. "Mr. Rogers—"

"Wade," he corrected, the deep, rich timbre of his voice spilling over and through her.

"Wade," she said and started her speech again, aware that her voice sounded calm despite the chaos going on inside her. "I think I might have left you with the impression that I was only being polite when I said you would be welcome at the Triple C anytime. And that isn't the case at all. If chance should bring you our way again, I do hope you'll stop."

"Do you mean that?"

"I do. Really."

"As it happens, I'll be in Montana the first of the week. I'd like to take you up on that invitation."

Cat gripped the phone a little tighter, conscious of the surge of gladness shooting through her. "I'll look forward to seeing you then." She flicked a glance at her father. "I'll give you back to my . . ."

"No need. Chase and I were finished. Tell him I'll see him next week. Bye, Cat."

97

"Good-bye." She handed the phone back to Chase. "He said he'd stop the first of the week."

Only a blind man would fail to notice the way Cat's eyes were shining, and Chase was not blind. Wisely he chose not to comment on it.

"I'm glad you told him we'd all welcome him," he said instead.

She gave him a narrowed look of sudden wariness. "Dad, when he comes, don't you dare start in with that husband nonsense again."

"I wouldn't dream of it. After all," Chase added with a barely suppressed smile, "we wouldn't want to scare him off, would we?"

"Dad!" Cat protested, all indignant.

"Don't worry. Your secret's safe with me." He pushed his chair back from the desk and collected his cane.

Cat opened her mouth to deny that she had any secret, then released all that righteous anger in a sigh and shook her head in amusement. "Arguing with you is hopeless."

She spun away and crossed to the doorway, meeting Trey on his way in with Chase's cup of cocoa. "I hope you'd like some hot cocoa, Gramps, because we fixed you a cup."

With the coming of the weekend, a warm front moved in, lifting the daytime temperatures into the forties and making conditions ideal for a trip into the foothills to find the perfect Christmas tree. Several candidates were located, but it was the one Jake picked out that they hauled back to the Homestead. Sunday afternoon was spent decorating it, with the whole family taking part, although Chase played more of a supervisory role.

Monday morning Cat awoke with a heady sense of anticipation. "First of the week," that's when Wade had said he would be stopping by again.

As she went about her daily routine, Cat kept one ear tuned to outside noises. The sound of a vehicle pulling up to the Homestead prompted a quick glance out a front window in hopes it might be Wade arriving. But Monday came and went without any sign of him.

When Tuesday morning turned out to be a repeat of the previous day, Cat finally faced the possibility that something had come up and Wade wouldn't be dropping by at all. Disappointment came, quick and strong.

With the entire afternoon ahead of her, Cat refused to let it hold sway. Instead she lifted her chin and squared her shoulders, silently chiding herself to stop acting like a schoolgirl. Behind her the dishwasher clicked into its next cycle. Absently she glanced around the kitchen.

Now that the noon meal was over, she virtually had the house to herself. Chase was in his room taking a nap. Jessy had gone back to the ranch office. Laredo had volunteered to run a part to an outlying camp, and Trey had taken charge of Jake so Sloan could make another trip to Wolf Meadow to track down a couple items on the inventory list.

Faced with all this free time, Cat decided to fill it by whipping up a batch of Christmas cookies. Twenty minutes later she placed the finished dough in the refrigerator to chill while she got out the rolling pin, cookie cutters, baking sheets, and parchment paper.

After dusting the countertop with flour, Cat started to put the nearly empty canister away, then changed her mind and decided to refill it first. As she went to take a new sack from the pantry shelf, she happened to notice there weren't any bags of powdered sugar on the shelf.

"Like it or not, I guess I'm going to the commissary for some sugar," Cat muttered to herself. "At least I discovered it before I started to make the icing."

She carried the sack of flour over to the canister. Just as she was about to pour it in, a voice came from the entryway, "Hello? Anybody home?"

It was Wade Rogers. She nearly dropped the flour sack. As it was, she spilled some of it on the counter. "I'll be right there!" she called back and hastily set the sack on the counter, then exited the kitchen at a running walk.

Cat found him in the entryway, as expected. He

was dressed much more casually than on his last visit, in a pair of blue jeans and an insulated vest over a blue chambray shirt. He smiled when he saw her, the action carving those sexy dimples in his cheeks and stirring up her pulse.

"I had decided you weren't going to be stopping by after all." Cat heard the breathy note in her voice, an echo of the fluttering excitement she felt inside.

"Sorry. I invited myself in." The deep timbre of his voice vibrated through her like a caress. "The last time I was here, Chase told me that only strangers knock."

"That's true. Welcome back." As she extended a hand to greet him, Cat noticed the dusting of white flour on it and hastily pulled it back to brush it away. "Sorry. I was in the kitchen doing some baking."

"In that case, I won't keep you. I don't want to be the cause of you ruining something. Is Chase in the den?" He gestured toward the room.

"Actually he's taking a nap. I'll wake him for you." She took a step in the direction of her father's first-floor bedroom.

A staying hand checked her movement. "Don't do that." He added a quick shake of his head. "I'll go outside and wander around a bit. Maybe check out that old barn, if that's alright?"

"Of course. Although—" Cat hesitated, then plunged on, hoping she didn't sound too forward,

"—as it happens, I need to go down to the commissary. I don't have enough powdered sugar to frost the Christmas cookies. Just give me a minute to get my coat and boots on and we can walk together."

"I'd welcome the company."

Cat had the impression he meant it, and the feeling smoothed away much of her uncertainty. He stood by while she pulled on her snow boots, then stepped forward to help her on with her winter coat. She murmured a "thanks." He acknowledged it with a nod, then opened the front door for her and followed her outside.

As they started down the porch steps, he said, "I'm guessing this commissary you mentioned and the ranch store my father told me about are one and the same thing."

"I'm sure they are," Cat confirmed. "We always keep it well stocked with basics as well as an assortment of other things.

"The Triple C prides itself on being self-sufficient. In its early days—before the advent of the automobile—it had to be. Now the commissary is more of a convenience."

"Sounds interesting. I think I'll come inside with you and check it out."

Cat tried not to let it show how pleased she was with his decision. As they angled across the ranch yard toward the store, she pointed out various buildings that comprised the Triple C headquarters, identifying everything from the structure housing the ranch offices, to the medical dispensary staffed by a registered nurse, and the fire station. Yet she never lost her awareness of him. If anything it was intensified by the occasional brush of his arm against hers. She tried to recall the last time she had walked side by side with a male who wasn't either a relative or a ranch hand, but she couldn't think of one. Not since Logan died.

"When an average Joe like me thinks of a ranch, the word conjures up images of barns and sheds, a bunkhouse, maybe even a cookshack," Wade remarked. "You have all those and more. You meant it when you talked about the ranch being self-sufficient."

"It's a necessity," Cat reminded him. "Outside help can be hours away."

Together they paused while a pickup bearing the ranch insignia pulled away from the gas pumps located outside the commissary. When it cleared their path to the door, they started forward again.

"I can see that now," Wade agreed and reached ahead of her to open the door. "But it's a hard concept to wrap your mind around until you are actually here."

"That's what everybody says." Smiling, Cat walked into the store and nearly ran straight into Laredo, who was on his way out. Cat stopped short, forcing Wade to do the same. "I thought you were running a part out to the West Camp."

"I am." His glance flicked past her to touch on Wade. "I decided since I was headed that way, I'd take their mail with me. Save them a trip." With the explanation made, he nodded a greeting to Wade. "See you made it back again, Rogers."

"That I did," Wade replied with an easy smile and came forward to stand next to Cat, extending a hand.

"Good to see you again, Laredo."

"Right." Laredo shifted the bundle of mail to his other hand and briefly gripped Wade's. "Come to do some shopping, did you?"

"No, I did," Cat inserted. "I need some powdered sugar. Since Dad was taking a nap, Wade came along with me."

"Cat's being my unofficial tour guide," Wade added.

"You couldn't be in better hands," Laredo stated, then stirred. "I'd best be on my way. Take care." He directed his parting words to Cat as Wade swung to one side, giving Laredo a clear path to the door.

Wade briefly tracked Laredo's departure with his gaze, then returned it to Cat. A crooked smile carved a groove into one cheek. "That's a hard man to read. He didn't seem surprised to see me—and he didn't seem all that glad either."

"That's just Laredo being Laredo." Cat

shrugged her lack of concern. "He tends to keep anyone he doesn't know well at arm's length. But he's the best thing that's happened to this family. Especially to Jessy."

"I know Chase definitely looks on him as family."

"We all do," Cat said with a smile and turned toward the aisle where the powdered sugar was located.

"Laredo said something about picking up the mail for the West Camp. I'm guessing that means the commissary serves as a post office, too."

"Yes, although unofficially."

Before Cat could explain her comment, Wade spoke. "Let me guess. The Triple C covers too many square miles for rural mail delivery to reach all of its corners, so the commissary is the clearing house for all personal mail that comes to its employees and their families."

"That's exactly right," Cat admitted.

"So what's this? Are you about to add a toy section for Christmas?" Wade motioned at the variety of toy items stacked high in a corner, some still in their original boxes.

"It looks like it, doesn't it?" she agreed on a laughing note. "Actually those are all donations for the Marines' toy drive. I think I heard Jessy say that they're scheduled to be loaded up tomorrow morning and delivered to the designated drop-off point."

"That's quite a haul."

"There wasn't a single person on the ranch who didn't contribute something toward it." Cat resumed her path to the powdered sugar.

"Full participation. That's really remarkable."

"I guess it is, but I learned long ago that cowboys have the biggest hearts."

"They certainly do on the Triple C." Wade paused next to her while she gathered up the largest sized bag of powdered sugar.

"So how do you usually spend the Christmas holidays?" Cat sent him a curious glance as she moved toward the back of the store and its counter area.

"It depends on where I am and what I might be in the middle of, although I always make a point to spend at least a couple days with my dad. Like Chase, he's up there in age so I can never be sure how many more Christmases I'll have with him."

"I know that feeling." And it warmed her to know that they had something in common.

"What made you ask?"

"Just curious," Cat answered with an idle shrug. "Some people like to laze on a tropical beach and others go skiing for the holidays. Me, I'm with the group that likes to stay home and spend Christmas with the family—and enjoy all the old traditions that go with it."

"Like iced Christmas cookies." He nodded in the direction of the powdered sugar she carried and flashed her a smile that carved those sexy grooves in his cheeks.

She laughed and admitted, "Cookies, caroling, and children's Christmas programs—the whole nine yards. Best of all, this year the house will be full of family. Jessy's daughter Laura and her husband are coming from England, and my son Quint is flying in from Texas with his wife and my new grandson. It will be the first time we've all been together in several years."

"Sounds fun," Wade remarked. "I guess that's one of the advantages of having a fairly large extended family. I didn't have the good fortune to be blessed with one."

Out of the corner of her eye, Cat spotted a new display of housewares and stopped to look, picking up a silicone rubber muffin pan. She read the label and tested its flexibility by bending it, balancing the bag of powdered sugar in the crook of her arm.

"What's that?" Wade asked.

"A muffin pan. They're supposed to pop right out."

He watched her for a moment until she put it back on the shelf and picked up a loaf pan, twisting that.

"I'll leave you to it," he said wryly. "And I'll go pick up some packaged snacks for the drive to the airport."

Wade wandered off and Cat took advantage of

the opportunity to examine the pans more closely, aware that she could use some new baking pans at the Homestead, especially with Christmas coming on.

Turning away from them, Cat mentally made a note to check which pans at the house needed to be replaced or supplemented. Absently she glanced up the aisle to the rear counter where the checkout was. As usual, Nancy Taylor was at the register. Nearing fifty and still sandy-haired, Nancy didn't fuss much with makeup or clothes, satisfied with lipstick and a simple combination of blouse and jeans.

Nancy's expression suddenly brightened with curiosity. Cat quickly realized that the object of her interest was Wade making his approach to the register.

"Can I help you?"

"I'm getting these." He set a handful of snacks in bright foil on the counter.

"Is there anything else you need today?"

"Don't think so." He glanced around as Cat joined him. "You ready too?"

"Yes." Cat felt the full force of Nancy's curiosity directed at her, as the other woman speculated on the connection between her and Wade.

"Hi, Nancy," Cat said, irritated by the touch of embarrassment she felt. "This is Wade Rogers. Wade, Nancy Taylor."

"Pleased to meet you, Mr. Rogers." She nodded to him, then noted the price of the sugar and bagged it for Cat.

"The Rogers folks are old family friends of Chase's," Cat stated, then hesitated, looking at Wade, hoping he would offer a further explanation.

"Oh, we go back years," Wade said vaguely.

"Isn't that nice." Nancy's tone was courteous but she seemed a little disappointed and Cat secretly didn't blame her for that. Wade Rogers was too attractive to fit the tame label of "family friend."

The other woman handed Cat a pen and a receipt for the sugar. "Please sign here."

"Thanks, Nancy." Cat jotted her name and they left.

Going out the door of the commissary, she turned to Wade. "Brace yourself. The ranch telegraph will be clattering big time."

"Because you bought five pounds of sugar?"

"No. Because I came in here with you. Around here, that counts as news."

"I'm flattered."

"Everyone will want to know who you are and what you're doing here, so you're liable to field a few questions." Cat sighed. "As will I."

Wade studied her with a sidelong glance. "Guess you don't do much dating, Cat." Startled, she lifted her head. He read the unvoiced question in her look and explained, "If you did, Nancy wouldn't have been so surprised to see you with a man."

Cat felt a little uncomfortable. "You're right." They were well away from the commissary by now, starting home across the expanse of the ranch yard. "Are you always so quick to read situations?"

"Oh, I've had a fair amount of practice. In my line of work, it's an essential skill."

"I imagine that's true," Cat replied.

They walked in companionable silence for a little while, Wade lifting his head to look up at the Homestead in the near distance, pillared and impressive.

"So, is it by choice?" Wade asked her.

Cat looked at him in confusion. "What?"

"That you don't date. Or date rarely. Whichever applies."

She really didn't want to answer that truthfully, but she did, her voice low. "By choice, I suppose. Although there is a definite shortage of eligible candidates."

"Especially ones brave enough to ask a Calder out."

Cat laughed. "You're underestimating the men who live in this wide-open land. Very little ever intimidates them." Pausing, Cat shook her head with wry amusement. "How did we get on this subject again?"

"Maybe because we're both wondering about it." Wade paused. "At least I am. I think you feel a similar attraction. If I'm wrong, just say so." He cocked his head. "Am I rushing things?"

"A little," Cat replied. "But I don't mind."

His expression turned rueful. "This whole dating scene baffles me. Things have changed so much. I feel awkward as hell. Like I lost whatever technique I might have had somewhere along the way."

The open confession disarmed her. "I know the feeling. I take it you haven't dated much either." She left the subject of the loss of his wife alone.

"No," Wade said. "I barely knew where to start. A couple of friends offered to fix me up, but I figured if I didn't click with someone they thought would be perfect for me, my friends would get insulted. So that wasn't an option. Then I looked into those online match-ups—" He shook his head with a grimace. "Not for me. How about you?" adding quickly, "if you don't mind my asking."

Cat laughed. "It's okay. I did the same thing one night when I was feeling lonesome."

"And?"

"I checked out the eligible men in my age range, but I didn't post a photo or profile."

"Maybe that's why I didn't find you," he teased.

"No. I quit looking before I signed up. Between grown men who posted their prom pictures from when they still had hair and all the oddballs who described themselves as 'fun,' I just wasn't interested."

He grinned. "Good."

"Besides that, it just seemed too strange to contact people I didn't know."

"I hear you. That's why I stuck with the old-fashioned methods. You know, strike up a conversation, get to know someone, take her out—" He smiled wryly but she felt a tiny flicker of jealousy.

Wade didn't seem to notice her lack of a reply. "I wouldn't say every date was an unqualified disaster, but there was no chemistry. Maybe I've been on the shelf too long."

"I don't think so."

"Thanks. Nice of you to say so." He gave her a warm look that made her pulse flutter. "Anyway, I just stopped looking. I guess I realized that I was doing it for all the wrong reasons. Maybe because I felt obligated to respond to invitations or because I was trying to get on with the business of living."

Cat could sympathize. "That's not easy after you lose someone you love."

His gaze became faraway and she regretted her comment, until he turned his focus back to her. "You know something? Right now if I didn't have to leave immediately after I speak with Chase, I'd be asking you to have dinner with me."

"And if you weren't leaving, I'd say yes." She drew in a breath, feeling like her old self again. A little headstrong. A lot flirty.

Wade looked at her intently. "Maybe you could give me a raincheck."

"Of course."

"It will be at least a week before I make it back, though," he warned.

"Fine. We can figure out the details then." She was feeling bolder by the minute.

"Not here at the ranch, though," Wade specified. "Somewhere else."

"The restaurant in Blue Moon is open again. That's the closest place to headquarters."

"That should work. Though I can't say I know where Blue Moon is."

"About an hour from here," Cat said. "Nothing up to D.C. standards, but I hear the food is good."

"That suits me."

A pickup truck honked behind them, the loudness and closeness of it startling Cat. She turned as it pulled up alongside them.

Laredo lowered the window and let the engine idle, leaning out to talk to Cat. "Thought I'd better tell you, Chase just called Jessy, wanting to know where you were, Cat."

"We're on our way to the house now."

"No need to call him back then." Laredo shifted out of park.

"No." She smiled and waved a good-bye. "Thanks, Laredo."

Cat started forward again with Wade at her side. They reached the porch as the pickup truck accelerated onto the main road of the ranch. At the front door, Wade reached around her to open it, then followed her inside. A second later Cat heard the familiar clump of Chase's cane.

He stopped, standing just outside his den. She couldn't quite decide if he was annoyed with her or not. His expression was impassive.

"Did you just get here?" he asked Wade.

The other man nodded. "I arrived a little less than an hour ago."

"I suppose you told him I was taking a nap," he said to Cat.

"I certainly did. It was the truth. I had to make a quick trip to the commissary for some powdered sugar and—"

Wade interrupted her. "I invited myself along."

Chase gave a thump of his cane as he turned. "After you put that sugar away, you can bring us some coffee, Cat."

She didn't mind his peremptory tone. Cat walked on air all the way to the kitchen, thinking about the evening she would be spending with Wade.

One week to wait. Already it seemed too far away.

Chapter 5

Sloan's trip to Wolf Meadow turned into a quick one. It was only mid-afternoon when she made it back to the ranch headquarters. Certain that Trey would appreciate a break from looking after Jake, she went in search of the pair. She finally found them in one of the machine sheds, taking apart a tractor motor. Trey was doing the greasy work, while Jake watched from the sidelines, clearly fascinated.

"Hi, Mom!" He jumped down from the metal footstool he'd been given to stand on.

"Hi, honey." She gave him a kiss and blew one to Trey, who was up to his elbows in black lube. He acknowledged the greeting with a lift of one greasy hand.

"Care to help?" he asked.

"No thanks. You're getting dirty enough for both of us." She ruffled her son's hair. "Having fun?"

"Yeah. Motors are cool. Dad was going to let me put part of it together."

"Aha. Then I'm just in time."

"Not from a little boy's point of view." Trey chuckled. "His hands are still clean."

"Let's keep it that way," Sloan stated, ignoring Jake's protest. Still he let her lead him away from the tractor without kicking up too much of a fuss. "See you later, Trey."

Absorbed in what he was doing, Trey nodded. "Sure thing."

Jake didn't stop talking during the short drive back to the house.

"Mommy, do you know what?" She didn't have to ask for the answer he supplied instantly. "I got to line up all the screws and count them. Dad said I got it different every time. Is that good or bad?"

Sloan laughed. "You'll have to ask your dad, but I'm glad you got to practice your numbers. Keep at it."

"I will. And then you know what?" Again he answered his own question. "Ralph gave me a big box of nails to sort by size. I put 'em in old jelly jars for him. Ralph sure has a lot of jelly jars. And a lot of nails, too."

"I'll bet he does. And I'll bet he was glad you helped him."

"Yeah," he said with satisfaction.

They pulled up in front of the house and parked by a car she didn't recognize, not noticing the rental agency sticker on the back bumper. Jake scrambled out and got down himself without waiting for his mother.

"Not so fast, young man." She got out and ran around the car to catch him by the wrist. "I think you're forgetting something you promised to do."

"What?" he asked innocently.

"As if you didn't know." They walked hand in

hand to the porch steps. One of Jake's sneaker laces had come untied but she wanted to get him inside the house first. "You have to rehearse for the Christmas play."

"Aw, Mom. I don't want to."

"That's not the issue. Everybody else in the Christmas play has to practice their parts, too."

"But it's a nice day," he said vehemently, as if that clinched the argument.

"It certainly is. In fact, it's a perfect day to rehearse a Christmas play."

"Aw, Mom," he grumbled, then sighed theatrically. "Okay, I'll do it."

"You don't have to act like you're doing me a big favor. When you commit to something like a play, you have to follow through. Remember, other children are depending on you. What if you stood up there and forgot your lines?"

"I'd make something up," he said confidently.

"That's not how it works—hey! Come back here!"

But he'd pried his hand loose and gone running in the direction of his great-grandfather's study. "I just remembered something I have to tell Greypa!"

"Jake—" Sloan stopped, her hands on her hips, looking after him with exasperation as he tugged open a door to the den and plunged inside. Hearing male voices from inside the room, she suddenly remembered the unfamiliar car outside and realized Chase had a visitor. On the heels of that, Sloan recalled Cat mentioning Wade Rogers intended to come back this week. Doubting that Jake's intrusion was all that welcome, she walked to the den to collect her wayward son. Sloan poked her head inside the room. A quick glance failed to spot him. "Anyone seen Jake?"

"He's right here," Chase answered.

Her son popped up from the far side of the desk like a jack-in-the-box. "I was hiding," he said mischievously.

"Now that you've been found, let's go practice your lines." Sloan motioned for him to join her.

"But—" he began in protest.

"That's enough of that. Run along like your mother said," Chase told Jake.

The little boy stood where he was on the other side of his great-grandfather's desk, playing with a pen he took from it. "Do I have to?"

"Yes. And you're interrupting," Chase said firmly. "That's not allowed." His glare was enough to take the steam out of Jake, who didn't argue as he handed back the pen and walked, crestfallen, to his waiting mother.

Sloan took his hand and turned around, reproving Jake in a low voice as they moved into the hall. He tripped over his untied sneaker lace. Halting, she knelt down and retied it, making sure it was double-knotted. "Shh. Greypa has work to do."

For a wonder, the little boy was completely quiet.

When she rose, a movement within the den caught her eye. Chase was handing Wade a piece of paper; it appeared to be the same size and shape as a bank check. Unwilling to give the appearance of prying, Sloan led Jake away from the den doors. Again he jerked his hand from her grasp and darted back to the den.

Sloan swore under her breath, took two steps at a time and reached the open door just in time to hear Chase say, "So you're set. There's more when you need it, of course. But this should smooth the way for you initially."

Jake was trying to hide behind the door where no one could see him. She uncurled his fingers from the doorknob and began to close it, saying in an almost inaudible voice that was more like a hiss, "You heard me. I said your great-grandpa is busy!"

"Who's there?" Chase called.

Sloan realized that both she and her son were outside his peripheral vision. "Sorry, Chase. Jake is being obstinate."

She moved into the doorway so the old man could both see and hear her well.

"Jake, obey your mother," his great-grandfather said. "No harm done," he added in an aside to Sloan. "We've just wrapped things up."

"That means the meeting is over," Jake said

knowledgeably, as if he attended them all the time. "I can go in."

Sloan shook her head. "You're going to your room. And I'm going with you. And you are going to study your lines until you have them memorized perfectly."

Chase smiled but his visitor tried not to. "Never argue with a woman when she's right, Jake. Now, quick march."

Jake scowled but he seemed resigned to his fate.

After the pair left, Wade turned to Chase. "I'd better be going. If you don't mind, I'll stop in the kitchen and tell Cat good-bye."

"Not at all. Keep in touch. And good luck."

"Thanks." Wade exited the den and started toward the rear of the house. As he crossed the living room, Cat emerged from the kitchen and saw him. She paused in mild surprise. "Are you two finished already?"

"We are. I was on my way to tell you goodbye before I left."

"Oh." Glowing, Cat seized the unexpected chance to have a private moment with him. "I'll walk you to your car."

In the entryway Cat grabbed a jacket that wasn't even hers. It wouldn't do to stand outside and shiver. By the time she had slipped it on, Wade had donned his coat as well. As if by mutual consent, they both moved toward the door. Again Wade opened it and stepped back to allow Cat to precede him. Cat had always considered herself as liberated as any modern woman, yet she still enjoyed the show of old-fashioned gentlemanly courtesy Wade displayed, finding it something to be savored.

The crisp winter air of late afternoon seemed to sharpen all her senses when she walked outside. She paused while Wade closed the door behind them and moved to her side, tucking a hand under her elbow to escort her to the steps.

"I could probably find my car, you know. But I really appreciate the company," he told her and added with a twinkle, "so walk slow."

Sharing the sentiment, Cat readily complied, postponing the moment when he had to leave.

"You won't forget about our date, will you?" he said in a light teasing tone as they negotiated the steps.

Smiling, Cat replied, "I made a mental note to add it to my social calendar the moment I'm back inside."

"Anyone else on that calendar besides me?" Pausing by his car, he opened the driver's door.

"I don't think so. But I'll have to check," she said impishly.

He chuckled. "You do that. I'll be seeing you." The warmth in his look promised that it would be as soon as he could make it.

She waved good-bye and stayed in the yard

until his car reached the main road, waving once more when he turned onto it, even though she knew he most likely couldn't see her.

Cat raced up the front stairs and peeled off the borrowed jacket the instant she was inside. She was filled with such a heady sense of anticipation, she had to resist the urge to hug it tightly to herself. Instead she crossed to the mirror in the front hall and examined her reflection, unaware that Chase had come out of the den. "Don't worry, girl," he said in a low voice. "You're still a beautiful woman."

Startled, she half turned to look at him. "You're prejudiced," she countered, but was still pleased by his compliment.

"And you're all starry-eyed," he observed thoughtfully.

"Is there a reason I shouldn't be?" The question was a lighthearted one but Chase recognized that it was her silent way of asking whether he knew something about Wade that she didn't.

"None at all."

"Good." She beamed at her father. "Wade asked me to have dinner with him the next time he came. I said yes."

"Ah," he said with a nod of understanding. "That must be why your smile reminds me of a kitten lapping up a saucer of cream. But a touch less innocent."

She laughed at his teasing.

"So." He leaned his weight on the cane. "What about those cookies? Did they get frosted?"

"Yes, they did."

He raised an eyebrow and looked upstairs. "I was going to see if that scamp Jake wanted to join me in the kitchen for some cookies and milk. Guess he must still be rehearsing his lines." As if on cue, Sloan started down the stairs, but without Jake.

"Where's Jake?" Chase asked her.

"He came down before I did," Sloan replied, automatically beginning a visual scan.

Chase looked around as well. "Not a trace of him. I wonder where Jake is," he said in a loud voice meant to flush his great-grandson out of hiding.

Silence.

"When he turns up, tell him that there are frosted Christmas cookies in the kitchen, Sloan," Chase said. "There might even be enough for him."

"I will," Sloan promised as Chase and Cat both headed toward the kitchen.

When she reached the bottom of the steps, Sloan paused, a little annoyed by Jake's disappearing act. She heard a noise coming from the den and walked down the hall to investigate. As she entered the room, Jake scrambled onto a wingbacked chair he had pushed up to the fireplace, and stood up on it. Balancing precariously, he strained to reach the set of mounted Longhorns above the mantel.

"Jacob Calder, you get down from there this minute!" She realized the second the words were out of her mouth that she'd startled him.

Jake wavered dangerously, then righted himself just in time to keep from crashing to the floor. He tumbled into the capacious seat, safe from a fall but not from his mother's anger.

"What were you doing?" She rushed to him. "You could have hurt yourself!"

"I just wanted to touch the horns."

He jumped down from the chair and ran behind the desk, knocking off some items onto the floor.

"Jake—" She sighed with exasperation.

He kept his distance, watching her with wide eyes that were suspiciously shiny and it occurred to her that he might cry if she yelled at him. Her irritation dissolved.

"Help me pick up the things on the floor," was all she said.

Jake obeyed, handing her Chase's flipped-open checkbook without closing it, more interested in a bubble-glass paperweight that fortunately hadn't been broken. He cradled its heavy smoothness in his small hands before he returned it to the desk.

Sloan wasn't paying attention. She was looking at the last check entry. Chase's handwriting on the stub was clear and bold.

To Wade Rogers. In the amount of ten thousand dollars.

Taken aback, she stared at the stub to make sure she'd read the amount correctly, wondering if it was for a charitable donation or what. But that space had been left blank.

Puzzled, she closed the checkbook and returned it to the desktop. "Aunt Cat made some Christmas cookies this afternoon. Your great-grandfather's in the kitchen. Shall we go join him for some milk and cookies?"

"Can I take the paperweight?" He cast one last admiring look at it on the desk.

"No. You don't want Greypa to know that you went tearing around and messed up the things on his desk, do you?"

The little boy squared his shoulders. "I'll tell him. He won't mind."

Sloan absently stroked his hair and smiled. "No, he probably won't."

"Jake's all tucked in and almost asleep." Trey walked into the master suite's sitting room, expecting to see his wife lounging on the couch. But Sloan was at the window, staring into the blackness beyond it, clearly preoccupied. "I thought you'd be watching television," he said, glancing at the darkened set. "Something wrong?"

"I was just thinking." She turned away from the window, still seeming distracted.

"About what?" Trey scanned her expression, sensing she was troubled about something.

Sloan hesitated to reply but she moved toward him. "I'm not sure," she said at first, then, "I guess I'm worried about Chase."

"Why?" Trey looked surprised.

"This afternoon Jake accidentally knocked some things off Chase's desk. His checkbook fell open—it's that old-fashioned kind, with four checks to a page, stubs on the left. I'm sure you've seen it."

"I have. So what about it?"

"The last stub was for a check he wrote to Wade Rogers. The checkbook was opened to it. I couldn't help seeing it," she added half defensively.

"So?"

"It was for ten thousand dollars, Trey. That's a great deal of money."

"What are you getting at?" Trey asked slowly, cocking his head to one side.

"Why would Chase write a check to Wade for such a large amount?" Sloan challenged. "He barely knows him."

"I have no idea." Trey shrugged. "Maybe it was a donation of some sort."

Sloan's mouth took on a grim, worried line. "Don't you think you should ask him about it?"

Trey drew his head back in surprise. "Why?"

Sloan took a few seconds to marshal her

argument before she responded. "Look, Trey, we don't know anything about Wade Rogers. Chase is getting old, and we have to be realistic about what that means."

Trey watched her. "I'm listening."

"Elderly people get tricked out of their money all the time. Con men specialize in frauds that target senior citizens."

"That's true," Trey admitted, and smiled his unconcern, "but Chase is way too wise to be taken in by such schemes."

"He probably has been in the past, but—"

Trey held up a silencing hand to stop her. "Look, it's his money. What he does with it is his business. I am not about to ask him to account for it."

Sloan's eyes darkened, their look matching her troubled frown. But she didn't shrug off the arm Trey slid around her shoulders. He drew her close, kissing her lightly on the forehead.

"Are you trying to distract me?" she asked softly.

"No. I respect your concern for Chase. But that check stub you saw doesn't worry me."

She looked up at him, not convinced. "I wish I felt the same way."

"Sooner or later, he'll probably tell us what it was for," Trey assured her. "Or not. It's up to him."

Sloan sighed and relaxed a little, leaning her head against her husband's chest, trying to absorb some of his confidence.

"Come on," he murmured, "let's go to bed."

Chapter 6

The winter afternoon was numbingly cold, even though the sun was shining. The crusty snow crunched under the hooves of the horses Jessy and Laredo were riding, revealing isolated patches of winter-brown grass where it had melted a few days before. Deceptively dull in color at this time of year, the native bunch grass was rich in nutrients that put hard weight on cattle, making it one of the ranch's best assets.

The riders were taking it slow as they surveyed the endless landscape that surrounded them. There was no sound but the occasional creak of saddle leather, or now and then a snort from one of the horses that made warm, rolling vapor rise in the air.

"Everything seems to be in good shape. Better than I expected, actually."

"You look happy, Jessy." Laredo ran an assessing glance over her profile, noting how relaxed and at ease she appeared without the stress lines that had been on her face when they set out. "You needed a break from the office."

Jessy admitted to that with a nod. "That's the one thing I don't like about running the Triple C," she said with a sigh. "I have to spend so much time inside four walls. I miss being out here on the land."

"You're not the only one," Laredo said.

She looked at him quizzically.

"I think Chase does too. He stays in his den most of the time. I remember when he rode out every day, rain or shine—or snow."

Jessy's expression grew sad. "Me too. It's a shame that his arthritis makes it impossible for him to sit in a saddle anymore. Seeing this land from inside a pickup cab just isn't the same as riding across it on a horse."

Laredo reined his mount to a stop, rested his gloved hands on the saddle horn and looked around. Jessy followed suit.

"There is one thing he's happy about, though," Jessy added as her horse sidled closer to his. "Cat and Wade Rogers hit it off."

"What makes you think that?" A trace of surprise was in his questioning frown.

"You mean you haven't heard all the clattering of the range telegraph?" she mocked lightly. "I guess they spent some time together the last time he was here."

"So. Is he sending roses? Or did he serenade her with an old guitar?"

"No serenades," she said. "He's a city slicker. They don't sing under windows in Washington, D.C., as far as I know. And he hasn't sent roses yet. But I understand they have a dinner date the next time he's here."

"Maybe it's time you and I went out to dinner,"

Laredo suggested after a thoughtful pause. "You haven't been off this ranch in a long while. Just the two of us, unchaperoned."

"It does sound good," Jessy conceded.

"Then what do you say we run into Blue Moon for dinner Friday night?"

"That's a date." Her eyes sparkled. "What time will you pick me up?"

"Seven o'clock," Laredo added. "And I'll be wearing my Sunday hat."

"Guess that means I should wear mine." Jessy reined her horse away and touched a spur to its flank. Laredo was quick to follow, lifting his horse into an easy lope.

In the dining room, Chase paused to survey the wide array of dishes and platters mounded with food that were spread on the long table.

"There's enough here for an army," Chase remarked. "Why so much?"

"I'm trying out some new recipes tonight. Not all of them might be to everybody's taste." Cat set down another steaming casserole.

"Looks damn good. And smells better. I might just help myself to extra servings," he joked. "How about you, Laredo?"

The lanky cowboy had crossed behind Chase's chair, but the old man didn't miss his entrance.

"I might give it a try. My momma used to say I had a hollow leg."

Jake played with the fork at his place setting. "Is your leg still hollow?" He stared at Laredo with new interest.

"That's just a figure of speech, Jake," Chase told him. "And don't ask me to explain what it means right now." He scanned the table. "Are we all here?"

Trey was the last to pull out a chair and take a seat. All bowed their heads while Chase offered a brief grace.

"Let's eat," he added after a heartfelt but quiet Amen.

Platters were passed and the food was dished onto plates. The eating and talking began. Seconds were offered, but when a platter of marinated roast beef came around to Laredo's seat for the third time he leaned back in his chair.

"Thanks, but I'm full. That was a good meal, Cat. Better than any restaurant."

"So why do you want to take me to one?" Jessy taunted lightly.

"Are you two going out somewhere?" Trey wondered.

"That's right," Jessy replied. "Laredo asked me out to dinner on Friday night, so don't set a place for us."

Trey looked over at Sloan. "Maybe we should plan a night out."

"Miles City?" she asked.

"Wherever you want to go."

Jake fiddled with a slice of beef on his plate. His mother leaned over to cut it into smaller pieces for him. "It's delicious," she told him. "Good Triple C beef, raised on the ranch."

He forked up a bite and nodded in agreement. After swallowing it, he wiped his mouth on his napkin and turned to Chase. "Greypa, how come none of our cattle have horns like the ones in your den?"

"Because that set came from a Longhorn steer," he replied. "Old Captain, he was called, born in Texas and led every herd Benteen Calder trailed north to Montana back in the Triple C's early years."

"Before I was born?" Jake asked.

"Before your great-grandfather was born," Trey said. "Can you believe that?"

"I guess so."

Chase threw him an admonishing look. "Don't make me feel any more ancient than I am, Trey." Redirecting his attention to Jake, Chase explained, "The Triple C raises Herefords and Hereford crosses now, instead of Longhorns."

"Oh. So are they astink?"

"What?" Sloan asked, puzzled.

"I want to know if the Longhorners are astink," Jake answered his mother patiently. "Astink like the dinosaurs," he clarified.

Chase chuckled. "The word is 'extinct,' Jake. And no, they're not. But you don't see too many

Longhorns these days, especially not in Montana."

"Why?"

"They like the weather in Texas better," his father answered.

"Wish we had one. With horns this wide." Jake extended his arms as far as they could go, then put them down again. "That'd be neat, huh, Greypa? I could show my friends, a real live one instead of just Old Captain's horns."

"They would be impressed," Chase agreed.

Jake's wistful words lingered in Chase's mind long after the meal was finished and the dining room emptied. A plan took shape, but Chase waited to implement it until Trey scooped up the sleepy-eyed youngster and nestled him against his shoulder.

"Bedtime for this guy," he said softly to Chase.

"I'm half-tempted to turn in myself. But I can't. You know, ranch business," he said vaguely. "Gotta make a few calls."

As Trey climbed the stairs with Jake, Chase crossed to the den and closed the door behind himself, going to his desk. He sat down and dialed a number he knew by heart.

"Quint?"

"Hey, Gramps. Nice to hear your voice," came the warm reply. "It will be even better when we can actually see you at Christmas time. We can't wait to get to Montana."

"Looking forward to it myself," Chase agreed. "How's Dallas? How's Josh? Never thought the day would come when there'd be a red-headed Calder running around."

Quint caught his grandfather up on his wife and toddler son, and then asked, "So how's everything up your way?"

"Everything's fine. But I need a favor."

"Sure. What is it?"

Chase got right to the point. "I want you to buy me a registered Longhorn calf. A bull calf."

There was a pause of disbelief on Quint's side of the call. "Did I hear you right? You want a Longhorn?"

"It's a Christmas present for Jake," he explained. "If you find one in time, you can have it shipped to South Camp. I'll let Stumpy Niles know it's coming. If it gets too close to Christmas before you find one, you'll need to fly it up in a cargo plane."

"Sounds like you have this all thought out," Quint marveled, faintly amused.

Chase grinned a grin that activated all his wrinkles, laughing. "I sure have. I stuck you with the hard part."

He raised his head when a knock came on the closed door. "Come in."

Cat opened it halfway and looked around the edge of the door. "Dad, are you busy?"

"Just talking to Quint." He spoke to his

grandson again. "Your mother's here. Want to talk to her?"

"Of course."

Chase gestured Cat into the room and handed her the receiver. He looked around for his cane and walked out slowly, still wearing that same grin.

Cat settled into the desk chair he'd vacated, happy to chat with her son. They exchanged small talk and he launched into a story about Josh's first kiss.

"What?" she said with surprise. "He's getting an early start. He's not two yet."

"Well, it wasn't exactly a kiss. More like bumping faces, very gently. But his little girlfriend didn't seem to mind. She didn't burst into tears or anything. Then Josh patted her hair."

"My, my," she said. "He's quite the charmer. Loved those last photos. Thanks for sending them, by the way."

"You're welcome. So how are you?"

She hesitated.

"I heard you're going on a date," he inserted on a teasing note.

"How'd you know that?" Cat said in surprise.

"We live in high-tech times, Mom. That famous Triple C ranch telegraph got a boost from e-mail."

"Oh." Cat tried to think of what to say, feeling a little chagrined that someone had told him before she could. "Well, yes. I do have a dinner date, but that's all. He's very nice. A friend of Chase's. About my age. His name is Wade Rogers."

"That's great, Mom," he said. "I'm really happy you met someone. And have fun. It's time you did."

They talked for a while longer, then said their good-byes. Cat hung up, staying in the chair for a bit, rocking and thinking. She hadn't known how to tell him, and she was glad that Quint was fine with the idea of her dating someone. Everyone seemed to be.

Like he'd said, it was time.

Chapter 7

A pickup truck with the Triple C brand painted on its doors jolted to a stop on a rough road that led to a small barn in South Camp. The barn was newer than the other outbuildings on the ranch, standing about a mile out from the main house.

"Sorry about them ruts in the road," the cowboy at the wheel said to Chase.

The old man looked down at the little boy beside him. "I'm all right. How about you, Jake?"

"I like going over bumps!" he said.

"That'll change when you're my age," Chase said wryly. He eased over on the seat after his great-grandson unlatched the door and jumped down. "Thanks, Eddy."

"No problem. I'll wait for you here."

Chase grasped his cane and took a deep breath.

"Need a hand gittin' out, sir?"

"Not yet. But that day is coming." Chase winced as he used the side of the truck for a handhold to get down. He leaned heavily on his cane once he was on the ground. "I don't trust my bad knee to a ranch truck clutch anymore."

"Not a problem. I'm happy to drive you. You two take your time," Eddy said. "I'll listen to the radio and roll one." He took a small pouch and papers out of his shirt pocket.

Chase shut the truck door and turned to follow

Jake into the barn. Back in the day, he'd done a regular walk-through of the stables and barns when he could, checking on the stock and the horses. It was one more thing that had slipped away from him. There was always the endless business of running the ranch to attend to, and then, before he knew it, his years had caught up with him.

Chase was determined to look over his operation thoroughly before the inevitable winter storms kept him housebound. He peered into the semi-darkness of the empty barn, hearing Jake's footsteps. "Jake? Don't go up in the hayloft."

"I didn't, Greypa! Here I am!" The boy came running toward him, full of energy.

"I see you. Settle down," Chase said, a fond note in his gruff voice.

Jake took the hand that wasn't resting on the cane. "How come you wanted to come here?" he asked. "The stalls are all empty."

"And that's good," Chase replied. "This is the barn for animals that need to be apart from the others because they're sick or lame. You know that."

"Yeah. Mommy let me watch the vet doctor a cow once. Can I be a vet when I grow up?"

"If you want to."

Jake ran off, climbing on a low stack of haybales and standing on top. "I can see into the stalls from here," he announced.

"How do they look?" Chase asked.

The boy peered around. "That one's full of fresh hay. The others don't have any."

Chase nodded. Everything was ready, per his orders. "We always keep a stall prepared, Jake. Winter's coming. Things happen. Now come on down."

Jake complied, pulling out a straw after he jumped off the last bale.

"Greypa, can I ask you a question?" He looked up, chewing thoughtfully on the straw.

"Sure." Chase leaned against the haybales, half sitting, half standing.

"One of the cowboys told me that the animals talk on Christmas Eve. Is that true?"

"I don't know. Could be," Chase replied indulgently. "Which cowboy was that?"

"Lavell—elli—" Jake shook his head. "I can't say it right."

"You mean Pete Lavelliere? The one from Canada?"

Jake nodded with relief. "That's him."

"Must be a story they tell up there."

Jake leaned on the bales beside him, unconsciously mimicking his great-grandfather's stance. "If a horse could talk, I wonder what he'd say."

Chase chuckled. "Oh, he'd complain that the cinch is too tight. And he'd ask right out for a carrot and never say please."

The little boy laughed at the idea and scampered off again.

"Where are you going?" Chase called.

Jake went into the stall with the hay. "Just checking," he called back.

"For what? There's nothing in there."

The boy came out again. "I wanted to see if there was oats in the nosebag or stuff like that. You said the stall was prepared." He paused for a beat. "Am I getting a pony for Christmas?"

"No. And don't start asking a lot of pesky questions. Christmas isn't just about what you're getting."

Jake looked a little ashamed. "I know. Mom said that too."

"Then you need to remember it," Chase scolded him gently. "You're going to get to be with your whole family this year. Aunts and uncles and even a baby cousin."

"Josh isn't such a baby anymore. He can walk now," Jake said happily.

"Better put any toys that you don't want him to play with out of reach," Chase advised him with a wink. "Come on. Let's go."

The pickup's high beams threw a tunnel of far-reaching light ahead of the vehicle, illuminating the edges of the ranch road and the dirty mounds of snow the plow had left behind. Moonlight glistened on the crusted surface of the snow that spread away from both sides of the road, the reflection of it stealing much of the night's blackness. Overhead a crescent moon looked down from the eastern sky, a scattering of stars surrounding it.

Just beyond the reach of the headlights, a set of darker masses loomed to flank the road. Laredo recognized the familiar shape of the east gate's stone-pillared entrance and eased his foot onto the brake pedal, slowing the vehicle's speed as it approached the intersection with the state highway.

There was a silky whisper of movement beside him as he slowed the pickup to a halt at the crossroads. He wasn't sorry to see a semitruck approaching from the south, forcing him to wait to pull onto the highway until it passed. He used the pause to steal a glance at Jessy, comfortably ensconced on the cab's passenger seat. The dimness of the dashboard's lights gave a faint sheen to the satiny material of the dress she wore and hinted at the paleness of a shapely calf.

"You do have a gorgeous set of legs," Laredo drawled the compliment. "And I'm glad you chose tonight to show them off."

"You did say you were going to wear your Sunday hat," Jessy reminded him, a smile in her voice. "Since you were making it a special occasion, I thought I should do the same." She stroked a hand over the skirt's smooth fabric. "And I have to say it feels good."

"I couldn't agree more." Laredo swung the pickup onto the highway and smiled to himself.

He suspected that most people—even longtime Triple C hands—would be surprised by Jessy's statement. The Jessy they knew was strong and steady, sure of herself and always in command. Very few even guessed she had a feminine side or that part of her might want to be regarded as a woman and not the boss of the Triple C.

"It's been a long time since I've taken you out to dinner, hasn't it?" Laredo realized. Usually they ended up at the Boar's Nest, the old line shack he'd fixed up to be a comfortable bachelor pad. It offered them total privacy, and most of the time that was all they wanted.

"We went out last fall," she reminded him.

"Just the same, we should do it more often."

"Maybe so, but life seems to get in the way a lot." A quiet acceptance of that fact marked her voice.

"You've got that right." His mouth crooked in a wry smile of agreement.

The dim glow of manmade lights grew visible a few miles ahead of them, offering the first sign of human habitation since they had left the ranch headquarters. Laredo slowed the pickup's speed as they approached the town of Blue Moon.

It was little more than a wide spot in the road with most of its buildings vacant since the coal mining operation had shut down. On the west side of the road, the combination convenience store and gas station sat in a bright pool of lights, a semi parked beneath its canopy next to a diesel pump. Directly across the highway from it was a restaurant and bar that had gone by many names in the past, but now proclaimed itself to be KELLY'S BAR AND GRILL.

"Marsha finally got her new sign installed." Laredo gestured in its direction.

"The lights are so bright, no one can complain about not seeing it." Jessy winced slightly at the glare.

"Probably LEDs," Laredo guessed and turned the pickup into the parking lot, which was already more than half full. "Looks like the Friday night crowd has already beat us here."

"Unless you want to drive all the way to Miles City, where else are you going to go?" Jessy reasoned, reaching for the door handle the instant the pickup rolled to a stop.

The sharp cold of the winter night made itself felt as soon as she swung down from the pickup's warm cab. Briefly Jessy wished she'd worn pants, then suppressed a shiver and moved briskly to link up with Laredo.

Together they struck out for the front entrance. Only when they reached the steps did Jessy slow her pace and run an assessing glance over the building with its lighted windows.

"I'm glad this place is back in the hands of a

local again," Jessy remarked in an idle, musing tone.

"I can't say I miss the clatter of all those slot machines Donovan had in here. Still . . . his selection of—shall we call them waitresses?—was rather easy on the eye." He grinned. "Or shouldn't I have noticed them?"

"As long as all you did was notice them, why should I care," Jessy returned smoothly.

Laredo laughed softly and opened the door for her.

A steady hum of voices greeted them when they walked in, punctuated by an occasional laugh or the crack of balls coming from the pool table area. Off to the side, a jukebox offered a country song with a two-step beat. Familiar faces were everywhere, some from the Triple C, others neighbors. Jessy recognized most of them; only those of the younger generation did she have trouble connecting to a name. She suspected it was merely one more sign she was getting older.

"Table or booth?" she asked Laredo, spotting a couple vacant ones of each.

"Booth," he said and guided her to an end one that offered them a semblance of privacy.

When they reached the booth, Laredo helped her out of her heavy winter coat and tossed it onto the booth seat, then shrugged out of his own while Jessy slid into the booth. A little too late, she remembered to gather up the material of her dress as she did, revealing a fair amount of thigh in the process.

"Move over," Laredo said and let his coat join hers on the opposite seat, then slid in next to her.

"We're going to look like a pair of teenagers," Jessy murmured, more self-conscious than actually embarrassed.

"When I'm with you, there are times when I feel like one," Laredo admitted, a caressing quality in a low-pitched voice intended for her hearing only.

Just for a moment she was caught up by the loving look in his eyes. She almost forgot they were in a room full of people. Then someone hailed her from across the way, snapping the spell. Jessy waved a response and reached for the menu propped behind the paper napkin dispenser.

"What are you going to have?" she asked.

"Steak. Like always. Medium rare."

Jessy looked up to find the waitress standing at their booth. "Might as well make it two."

After they had given the waitress their order, Laredo stretched an arm along the back of the booth behind her and angled himself toward her.

"Did I tell you that I've figured out where I want to put the hot tub you're getting me for Christmas?"

"You're serious about this, aren't you?" Jessy realized with a small, amazed laugh.

"You mean you haven't bought it yet?" he

chided mockingly. "It doesn't have to be anything gigantic. Something just big enough for two."

"That's a relief."

"Christmas isn't very far away. You'd better get to shopping," Laredo warned.

"Tell me about it. I still haven't gotten anything for Sloan."

"Mind if I make a suggestion?"

Jessy started to say "yes," then hesitated. "I don't think she wants a hot tub, too."

"No, I agree." His expression grew serious. "But there is one thing that would mean a lot to her."

"What's that?"

"The Calder family Bible."

She was immediately struck by the rightness of his choice. Her daughter-in-law had grown up an orphan, without a place she could call home or any relatives like Laredo. And who else but Laredo would know how empty life could feel without a sense of belonging somewhere.

"You could get her some other little something besides that, but—" Laredo began.

"You're right. The Bible is the perfect main gift for her." Jessy nodded in satisfaction, then gave him a sideways glance. "So what are you buying me?"

Laredo pulled back. "That's a surprise."

"You can give me a hint at least."

They bantered back and forth on the topic until

the waitress returned with their drinks and meal order. After that, talking took a back seat to the business of eating.

They had almost finished their steaks when Ross Kelly stopped by their booth. "How are the steaks? It's Calder beef so they should be good."

"They're delicious," Jessy assured him. "I don't know what you used for seasoning—"

Ross held up a warning hand, a big grin splitting his face. "And I'll never tell, so don't bother asking. It's my own secret recipe."

"Spoken like a true chef." Laredo half-rose in greeting, extending a hand to Ross who shook it.

"I'm working at it." Ross cleared the end of the opposite booth seat and perched his wide-hipped frame on the outer edge of it after darting a quick glance at the kitchen to make sure he wasn't needed.

"Doesn't sound like you've started missing being on the road," Jessy guessed. "After a couple years operating this place, I thought you might get homesick for it."

"Not a chance," he declared. "Cooking has always been something I loved doing. And with diesel prices being what they are, a man can't make good money anymore driving a truck. This place came up for sale at the right time for Marsha and me."

"From what I heard, the court-appointed lawyer

for Donovan's estate practically paid you to take it," Laredo jested.

"We got a good deal on it," was the most Ross would admit.

They chatted a bit about the business. All the while Ross kept one eye on the kitchen area. Somewhere in the conversation Jessy got the sense that Ross hadn't stopped by their booth merely to make sure the food was all right—or to be social. He had some other reason.

As she was trying to figure out what it might be, Ross leaned forward in a confiding manner. "I'm glad you stopped in here tonight, Laredo. A couple weeks ago I hired a new guy to work in the kitchen. A Mexican named Octavio. He's been asking about you."

"Really? Why?" Laredo's tone was smooth but wary.

"Damned if I know," Ross admitted. "But he knows your name and he knew you live in this area. Just not where."

Stiffening a little, Jessy stole a worried glance at Laredo, not sure what any of this meant, but she had a feeling it wasn't anything good.

"Did he say what he wants with me?"

"Not to me. But one time I did overhear him talking about you in Spanish to Miguel. Octavio mentioned your name and then said something about being sent by the wind. I probably got that part wrong, but that's what it sounded like."

"The wind, huh." Laredo smiled. And it was the ease of his smile that Jessy immediately noticed. All that innate wariness was suddenly gone. "Now you've got me curious. If it's all right with you, I'll go talk to him and find what all this 'wind' business is about."

"Sure. I'll take you back."

The two men eased out of the booth and Ross walked with Laredo to the rear of the restaurant, not far from their booth. Shifting in her seat, Jessy watched as Ross went into the kitchen and came out with the Mexican. After introducing him to Laredo, Ross left the two men alone.

She strained to hear what was said. Octavio's voice was low and he spoke in rapid-fire Spanish that she didn't understand. Laredo's first words were clear.

"Slow down. My Spanish is a little rusty." She made out that much in a lull in the restaurant noise.

Octavio appeared to comply, but a party of five came in, talking among themselves and calling out greetings. There was no way Jessy could hear Laredo's conversation above their noise. She gave up trying and simply waited.

After a few moments more, Laredo returned to the booth.

"What was that all about?"

"Nothing, really." He slid onto the seat beside her. "Sorry it took so long."

Not buying his answer, she pressed for a better explanation. "It had to be more than nothing."

"He's just a friend of a friend, up here looking for a job."

"Ross said he was working for him."

Laredo nodded and checked out the dessert menu. "Yeah, but he'd like something with better pay."

"Why is that your problem?"

"It isn't," he said absently. "That chocolate cake looks good. Or maybe I'll have a slice of pie." He glanced up at her, his gaze shuttered. "But I don't mind vouching for the guy if he wants to hire on as a cook somewhere."

"You mean the Triple C?" Jessy frowned.

"No. As far as I know, Baker doesn't need any extra hands."

Jessy wasn't fooled by his casual tone. But if he wasn't going to tell her what really had been said between him and the stranger, she had no way to drag it out of him.

"Okay. Whatever you say, Laredo."

His withdrawn expression made her uneasy, that and his air of preoccupation, a kind of odd thoughtfulness. There was one possible cause for both.

"Is something wrong?" She watched him closely.

He put down the menu and looked at her. "No. Not at all. I was just remembering—"

"What?"

Laredo shrugged and smiled. "The old days. Before you." His gaze was warm, almost adoring.

She had the impression that he was studying her carefully. As if he was memorizing every feature of her face. But she couldn't detect anything that suggested Laredo was troubled by the meeting. Maybe he had been simply recalling his past life. Did he miss it? Or someone. Sitting side by side when he was a million miles away was frustrating.

"To the Boar's Nest? Takes a while to heat up that old line shack, but there is plenty of firewood."

"The ranch, then. We don't have to go in to the main house. I just want to be somewhere alone with you. We don't have to talk either."

"I like the way you think." He retrieved an ancient hand-tooled leather wallet from his jeans pocket and took out several tens, sliding them under the condiments holder where the waitress could see them.

"Thanks for dinner." She smiled at him.

"Any time."

Eventually, they pulled over on one of the ranch's back roads and just held each other for a long time, doing more kissing than talking. There was a sweet intensity to his strong and slow lovemaking that Jessy had been missing lately. At the same time his gentle caresses made her crave more from him, but they could only go so far in the cab of a pickup on a winter night.

Laredo lifted his head and glanced out and around, as if he was checking their surroundings. The immense landscape stretched empty to the black edge of the horizon.

"Look at that," Laredo said.

Jessy moved out of his embracing arms and saw the crescent moon above them in the clear night sky, shining from within a vast, delicate circle of ice high in the atmosphere.

"It's beautiful," Jessy murmured in wonder. "Something you don't see very often."

"Maybe it's a sign."

She turned to look at his shadowed face. He wasn't smiling. "Of what?"

He gave a short, low laugh. "If you asked Chase, he'd say it meant bad weather was on the way."

"Probably." Jessy smiled in agreement. "What does it mean to you?"

He didn't reply right away. "Can't exactly say what it means," he said after a while. "Maybe that we ought to stop what we're doing and look up more. And give thanks for what we have as long as we have it."

"What are you getting at?" The tinge of melancholy in his comment confused her.

"I can't explain it, Jessy. Not now." He pulled her back into his arms and kissed her with a sudden, fierce hunger that left her wonderfully breathless.

Chapter 8

Sloan came down the oak stairs, balancing an armload of wrapped gifts. As she rounded the newel post at the last step, she inadvertently bumped against it. One package teetered. She did a little juggling act and managed to keep it from falling. There was no one around to hear her sigh of relief. She'd wanted to get the gifts wrapped and under the tree before a certain curious kid knew what his mother was up to.

Not that the presents were all for Jake. But he was apt to think so. She didn't want any of them rattled or poked or subjected to a small boy's mental X-rays.

Hoping he wasn't hanging out with his great-grandfather in the den, Sloan made a detour to the room's open door, catching a glimpse of Chase at his desk, absorbed in paperwork.

So far, so good. As quietly as she could, she retreated to the living room where the tree was. Carefully, she set the presents down beside it, then took a minute to arrange them around the skirted base.

Finished, Sloan stepped back to admire the ever-growing pile. Recalling how many already had Jake's name on their tag, she reminded herself to have a notepad and pencil nearby for a thank-you list. If nothing else, Jake was going to sign his name to the card to acknowledge each and every one of his gifts.

As she started back to the stairs, she heard Chase talking. It took a second for her to realize he was on the phone with someone. Drawn by the intensity in his deep voice, Sloan paused to listen.

"Sounds like you're making progress," Chase said to whoever was on the other end of the line. "Can't come quick enough. Time's getting short."

There was a long pause while he listened. Sloan stayed where she was, feeling a twinge of guilt that she was eavesdropping on a private conversation.

"As soon as you give me the word, I'll have it ready," Chase went on. "Yes. It's already arranged."

She hesitated as Chase wrapped up the call.

"Stay in touch, Wade."

The minute she realized Chase had been speaking with Wade Rogers, she recalled the check Chase had written to him. The telltale creak of the desk chair followed by the clump of the cane warned Sloan that Chase was getting up. Not wanting him to find her, she moved quickly and noiselessly back to the Christmas tree.

By the time he emerged from the den, she was occupied with bending the thin wire hook on a bauble and re-hanging it on a different tree branch.

His sharp gaze traveled over her with a thoroughness that made her quail inside. Then his attention shifted to the wrapped presents. "Either my eyes are deceiving me or that heap is growing higher. You must have added more."

"A few." She nodded, fighting an attack of nerves. "I did."

"Aha. I thought I heard you come downstairs. Having fun playing Santa Claus, are you?"

"Always," she said with a quick smile. She was relieved that he didn't suspect her of eavesdropping, but that didn't make her feel less guilty about it. "I wanted to get them out of hiding while Jake is over at Dan's house playing. He should be back any minute."

"I wondered where he was."

"I have nearly everything wrapped and one batch under the tree. So far, I'm in good shape."

"Indeed."

Sloan didn't know whether to stay or leave. Chase was looking at her as if he expected her to say more. Overcome with curiosity, she decided to ask him about the call. It wasn't as if he'd had his door shut.

"Did I hear right? Were you just on the phone with Wade Rogers?"

"I was. Why do you ask?"

She attempted an idle shrug. "I was just wondering if he told you when he would be back. I mean it's so very obvious how much Cat is looking forward to having dinner with him."

The remark, meant to distract him, worked. His

pleased expression told Sloan that much. "Yes, she is anxious." Then he remembered her initial question. "If all goes well, Wade should be here this weekend."

"Just in time for the ranch Christmas party."

"Forgot about that," he said. "It's this Saturday, isn't it?"

"Yes, although I can't say Jake's looking forward to playing the shepherd boy."

Chase gave a chuckle. "Still grumbling about wearing those sandals, is he?"

"Only all the time. Oh—" The bauble she'd hung slipped off its pine twig and went rolling. Sloan knelt behind the Christmas tree to look for it. "Darn, I think it went under the bookcase," she said to Chase.

Bending low, she slid a hand under it but found a dust-bunny instead of the missing ornament.

The front door opened and Laredo called out, "Anybody home?" as he came in.

"In here," Chase replied.

Laredo's long stride carried him to the living room, and he spotted Chase. "Just the man I'm looking for—" He broke off in surprise when Sloan scrambled to her feet, brushing her hands on her jeans. "Hello, Sloan."

"What do you need?" Chase asked.

Laredo's glance lingered on Sloan. "Just wanted a word with you. Nothing important." He half turned. "I'll catch you later."

Sloan had the definite impression that her presence was the cause of his sudden change of plans. "Don't leave on account of me. I still have a bunch of gifts upstairs that need to be wrapped, believe it or not. You two go have your talk."

She followed through on that tactful exit line by crossing to the staircase, leaving the pair alone. Laredo tracked her progress while Chase took the opportunity to study him in silence. The other man's impassive expression didn't tell him much. But Chase was well aware that if Laredo wanted to speak to him in private, it had to be about something serious.

"Let's go in the den," he suggested. Laredo walked behind him for the short distance, slowing his steps to match Chase's, until the older man reached his desk and settled into his seat. "Close the door."

Laredo did, then turned back, his mouth set in a hard line as he met Chase's probing glance.

"So what's the problem?"

Laredo didn't immediately answer. Instead he went to a front window and looked out. "I'm not sure. But I may have to leave here. If I do, this is about as much notice as I can give you."

"Why?"

He swung away from the window, but kept to the side of it. "Last night a friend sent me a warning that my name's become a topic of discussion—in places where it hasn't been mentioned in years."

"Who told you that?"

"No one you know. Jessy doesn't know about this, and I'd prefer that she didn't."

Chase's gaze was steady. "She won't hear a word of it from me." He paused for a beat. "Laredo, I won't argue. You may have good reason to be leery. But the Triple C is the safest place you can be."

Laredo didn't seem convinced.

"It may be wise for you to drop out of sight, but you can do that here. No one on this ranch will ever tell anyone where you are."

"Still . . ." He didn't finish the sentence.

"Ever try to search a million acres for someone? That's how big this ranch is," Chase reminded him.

"I know that. But I'd just as soon not put any of you in that position."

"That's not your choice to make," Chase stated. "Let's play it on the safe side for the time being, and arrange for you to stay away from headquarters for a while."

Laredo gave an uncomfortable shrug. "Jessy will want to know why."

"I'll handle Jessy."

"How?"

"Easy," Chase replied. "I'll simply explain that you're taking care of some personal business for me. She may wonder, but she won't question that."

"It might work," Laredo conceded.

"Of course it will. Now—we need to figure out the best spot on the ranch for you to lie low. You can't go back to the Boar's Nest. Too many people know that's your bachelor quarters."

Laredo thought a moment. "What about Wolf Meadow? I could stay at Buck Haskell's old place there."

Chase shook his head. "Too hard for me to reach you if I need to. The Shamrock ranch will work better."

"O'Rourke's old place?" Laredo asked. "What kind of shape is the house in?"

"Can't be any worse than the Boar's Nest," Chase pointed out. "And like your place, it can't be seen from the road. Trey was over there last fall and fired up the generator to make sure it was still in working order."

Laredo nodded in approval. "Sounds good. I'll grab some clothes and supplies and head that way."

He turned to leave but Chase stopped him with an upraised hand. "If I need to get in touch with you, I'll send Trey and only Trey. If anyone else shows up, you'll know they aren't from me."

"Thanks, Chase." Laredo put a lot into those two simple words.

Chase waved off the expression of gratitude.

"You've had my back more times than I care to count. It's time I covered yours. With any luck, this will all blow over before Christmas."

"Let's hope so." Laredo walked out.

When lunchtime came, Chase made sure he was the first one to take a seat at the table. Jessy was among the last to arrive, walking in as Cat placed the last of the food dishes on the surface. She halted in the doorway and made a quick scan of the faces at the tabletop.

"Has anyone seen Laredo?" she asked. "I thought he'd probably beaten me here."

Quick to play on the excuse of his advanced age, Chase feigned a frown of both surprise and apology. "Did I forget to tell you Laredo's going to be gone for a while?"

"Gone?" Jessy repeated in astonishment. "Where?"

"That's my business." Chase shook out his napkin and laid it across his lap.

Hands on her hips, Cat gave him a reproving look. "Dad, don't tell me you've conned Laredo into doing some Christmas shopping for you? First Quint and—"

Chase cut her off. "Just never you mind about what he's doing or why. This isn't the time of the year to be getting nosy and asking a lot of questions."

Out of the corner of his eye, he observed the

161

way Jessy visibly relaxed at hearing his response. At the moment, he knew she was satisfied there was nothing wrong.

"How long will he be gone?" Jessy walked over to her customary chair at the table and pulled it out.

"Does it matter?" Chase countered.

"Not really," she said with unconcern. "I was just wondering if I'd have time to get that hot tub installed before he gets back."

"What hot tub?" Chase frowned.

"The one he wants for Christmas," Jessy replied.

"That should work out perfectly for you then," Chase said, "because I don't expect him back at the ranch until right before Christmas."

"He'll be gone that long?" Jessy glanced at him in surprise.

"You make it sound like forever," he chided lightly. "Christmas is only a couple of weeks away."

"Is 'Redo going to buy me a present?" Jake asked eagerly.

"Should he?" Chase turned the question back on him. "Are you buying him one?"

Gripped by uncertainty, Jake turned to his mother. "Are we, Mom?"

The question drew soft laughter and diverted the conversation away from any further discussion of Laredo's absence. Which was exactly what Chase wanted.

The one-hundred-plus-year-old barn was a hive of activity, undergoing its annual transformation into a site worthy of a Christmas gathering. Those ranch hands assigned to tasks were on tall ladders hanging red and green crepe paper from the rafters while wives and older members of their families adorned the stalls with evergreen garlands and holiday wreaths.

Sloan stood at the base of one ladder, holding it steady while high above her Tank Willis twisted red and green crepe paper together to form a double garland, then held one section of it to the rafter.

"Thank God for staple guns," Sloan declared.

He grinned at her. "That's how the West was won. Of course, back then it was barbed wire that was getting fastened to a post." He picked up his gun from the small tool shelf on the ladder and pressed it against the end of a garland, banging staples loudly into the rafter.

Startled by the sudden, explosive sound, Cat jerked her head up, realized what made it, and muttered to herself, "Noisy things."

"How's the wall decorations coming?" someone hurrying by asked.

"Just fine," she said to the woman's back and returned to sorting through boxes, trying to find all the pieces to a pin-the-nose-on-the-reindeer game.

Bright sunlight briefly flooded the wide central alley when its big door was swung open. Cat looked up to see who entered, hoping it was Wade. But it was one of the ranch hands carting another box. She took a moment to survey the progress that had been made. For the most part they seemed to be on schedule.

Food that didn't need refrigerating, mostly sweets, was already set out on a long table, protected by plastic wrap. There were several platters filled with gingerbread cowboys and sugar-cookie cowgirls, their shirts and jeans outlined in colored icing with silver dragées for the snaps. Cat suspected they were the handiwork of Kelly Taylor. But whoever made them, they looked too good to eat.

In the stage area, the children were rehearsing the play in their everyday clothes, working off energy by teasing each other and dashing around the platform. Babette Nevins, who was in charge, looked to be having a tough time of it.

Cat thought about lending a hand, but she wasn't sorry when Sloan came toward her with beaded garland draped in layers over her arm.

"Cat, these will need to go on the tree first. Can you help me loop them around? I don't think I can manage it by myself."

"Sure." Cat quickly closed the flaps of the big box at her feet. "Look at those gorgeous colors."

"Purple and gold." Sloan laughed. "Not very

traditional, but I guess we have enough red and green around here. The little girls will love them though."

"They seem to love anything with purple in it," Cat agreed and followed Sloan the short distance to the tree.

Sloan walked around the legs of a tall ladder. A strand of crepe paper drifted in front of her face, and Sloan blew it away.

The tree stood well over ten feet tall in its holder. Freshly cut two days earlier, it gave off a pine scent that overpowered the barn's normal smells. "We're going to need a step ladder for this," Sloan observed.

Cat spotted one across the way and went to drag it over. On her return, she found Sloan seated on the floor pulling more rope garlands from a bag and draping them carefully over her jeans-clad legs.

"You're younger. You can do the climbing." Cat pressed down on the side braces to secure the ladder.

"No problem." Sloan gave Cat at least ten strings of purple and gold beads, and rose from her seat. "If you could hand me those, we can start at the top of the tree and work down."

"Sounds like a plan to me."

Cat waited at the base of the ladder and handed Sloan the garlands one by one. Some hung in perfect loops, but a few slithered down through the branches and rattled onto the barn's brick-paved floor. Sloan's muttered swearing made Cat laugh.

At first Sloan didn't think it was amusing but in the end, she had to laugh as well. "Why did I sign up for this?" she said with a mock groan.

"I don't know, Sloan. Did you get more presents?"

"No. Damn!" Another garland slithered down into the bucket. "I guess we can fish those out when we're done." She concentrated on her loops and got the top half of the tree done. Sloan stepped backward down the ladder, pausing to assess the job. "Not bad. Actually, I think I can do the rest myself from here on in. Don't you want to get ready?"

"For what?" Cat gave her a puzzled look.

"More like for whom. Wade's coming, isn't he?"

"He's supposed to," Cat admitted. "But I don't know when he's arriving exactly. Chase wasn't specific."

"Oh. Do you think he will stay for the ranch party?"

"I don't know that either." Cat smiled up at the young woman on the ladder. "If he does or doesn't, it won't really matter to me. Just as long as he comes."

Sloan went down the final few steps and stood on the floor. "You should see your face, Cat. You're all flushed just thinking about him."

Cat gave her a self-conscious look. "It's warm in here."

"Of course." Sloan quickly accepted the excuse rather than embarrass Cat further. She cast a glance at the men coming down from their ladders, finished with hanging the red and green crepe paper. "Look at that. They did a great job. Even without Laredo to supervise."

The mention of Laredo prompted Cat to wonder, "What do you suppose Dad has sent him off to buy?"

"I don't even have a good guess," Sloan admitted.

"Neither do I, especially when I think of what Dad asked Quint to get Jake."

"What?" Sloan fixed her with a wary look. "Is he having him buy something I wouldn't for Jake? Please tell me it isn't a drum set."

"I promise it isn't a drum set," Cat assured her. "But I'm not going to say any more than that. It's better if you don't find out ahead of time."

"That is not reassuring," Sloan declared, then tipped her head to one side.

"But, if he sent Laredo to fetch a Christmas gift, it really makes me wonder what it is and who it's for."

Cat shrugged. "Who knows? Dad is definitely thinking outside the box this year."

"Okay. I'll stop pestering you." Sloan smiled. "Oops—almost forgot." She kneeled at the bottom of the tree and gathered up the garlands that had fallen to the floor. "They're all dusty."

"I'll get a rag or something." Cat laughed and went to fetch one from the same closet the ladder came from. Sloan waited for her, wondering briefly about that outside-the-box comment.

If the ten-thousand-dollar check Chase had given to Wade was for a Christmas present, it had to be one hell of a big one. She couldn't imagine what it might be. But then Chase could be awfully close-mouthed about his financial affairs. Maybe Trey was right and it was a charitable donation or something else that wasn't remotely festive.

She put the thought aside as Cat returned, a towel in hand. Cat held it like a hammock and Sloan poured the dusty beads into it.

"Anything else in the bucket?" Cat asked.

"I don't think so." Sloan rolled the strands around in the towel. "So what were you doing when I came over?"

"Sorting out the wall decorations."

"I'll give you a hand."

"Around four o'clock" had long been the stated starting time for the Triple C's ranch party for its employees. As usual, the first arrivals showed up at the big timbered barn shortly after three. Those from distant corners of the ranch left early in case the roads were bad. Others, especially the bachelors, were all cleaned up for the party and had nothing better to do.

From her bedroom window, Cat could see the steadily growing collection of vehicles parked at the barn. Any other year she would already have been at the barn by now as well. But this year she hadn't left the Homestead when Jessy, Trey, Sloan, and Jake had. Cat had used the excuse that Chase wasn't ready and that she would stay to drive him to the barn later.

All knew that Chase wasn't ready because he was waiting for Wade Rogers to come—just as they knew Cat was staying for the same reason.

Aware that she had dawdled in her room long enough, Cat selected a pair of earrings from her jewelry box and crossed to the mirror to put them on. She gave her reflection a cursory glance. The bright red of her Christmas sweater jarred her, making her realize how far from festive she felt.

"You might as well face it," she told the woman in the mirror, her voice tight and low, "you've been stood up."

The words twisted through her like a knife for a moment. She shut her eyes in an attempt to check the sharp ache, then determinedly shook off the hurt, her chin pitching forward at a proud angle.

"No," she told herself. "He simply wasn't able to make it today."

As she fastened on the last earring, she caught the rumbling sound of a vehicle outside. A second later, Cat realized that she could hear it so clearly because it was directly out front.

Wade?

Pushed by a fresh surge of hope, Cat flew to the window, reaching it as Sloan stepped out of the driver's side and headed for the front steps. Abruptly she swung away from the window, squared her shoulders, and left the bedroom, head high.

At the top of the staircase, Cat saw Sloan on her way up, taking the steps two at a time. It was the angry set of Sloan's features more than her haste that caught Cat's attention.

"What's wrong?"

"That Jake," Sloan muttered. "I had his costume all together in a tote. After I got to the barn, I discovered his sandals were missing and I happen to know they were in there —right on top."

A laugh bubbled in Cat's throat. She fought it down. "He hid them."

"I'll find them and he's going to wear them if I have to—" Sloan left the rest of the threat unfinished and headed for her son's bedroom.

"Check his pajama drawer," Cat called after her. "That's where Trey put things he didn't want Jessy to find."

Sloan halted halfway through the doorway and threw Cat a puzzled look. "The pajama drawer? Why there?"

Cat shrugged. "Who knows how a little boy's

mind works? But would you have looked in his drawers?"

"Only if I couldn't find the sandals anywhere else. Thanks." Sloan swung back into the bedroom and crossed directly to the chest of drawers.

Cat didn't wait to see if Sloan found them there but went down the stairs in search of her father. As expected, she found Chase in the den, seated behind his desk, an elbow propped on the chair arm with the knuckles of a fisted hand idly tapping his mouth. Impatience was in his expression as he contemplated the scene beyond the den's window.

Cat paused in the doorway. "It's nearly four o'clock, Dad. Time for us to join the party."

He grumbled a non-response and lowered his hand as he let his gaze slice to her. "Why was Sloan in such a hurry?"

"She had to come back for Jake's sandals," Cat replied and took the first step toward the front entry. "I'll go start the car while you get your coat on."

She retrieved her own parka from its wall hook, dug out her leather gloves and slipped them on. As she dipped a hand back in the pocket for the car keys, Cat heard the clumping of Chase's cane that said he was following her.

Keys in hand, she stepped outside and turned back to close the door behind her, breathing in the invigorating crispness of the late afternoon, glad to find that the temperature wasn't brutally cold. As she crossed the columned veranda to the steps, she focused her attention on separating the ignition key from the others on the ring. It wasn't until she reached the top of the steps that Cat noticed the man standing at the bottom of them.

"Wade—" She breathed his name in stunned surprise.

She didn't even realize she dropped the keys until she heard the jangle of them hitting the steps. Before she could recover, Wade was bending to pick them up for her.

"Were you headed out to search for me?" The twinkle in his dark eyes was teasing. But Cat had a hard time seeing it; she was too absorbed by the caressing way his gaze moved over her face.

"Actually, I had decided you weren't going to be able to make it today," she admitted, still feeling a little breathless.

"I almost didn't. It was one weather delay after another." He offered the keys to her, coming up a step as she moved down. Rather than release the keys when her gloved fingers closed around them, Wade continued to hold them. "I guess that always happens when you're eager to get somewhere."

He came up one more step, and their faces were level with each other. Cat tipped her head fractionally in the age-old way that invited his kiss. He seemed about to comply when the front door opened behind Cat and the end of a cane stomped on the veranda's wooden floor. Wade's head lifted and Cat turned, frustrated by the sight of Chase.

"Wade. You're here." The words were barely out of his mouth when Chase shot her an impatient glance. "Why didn't you tell me, Cat? You know I've been waiting for him." He didn't pause for a response. Instead, he opened the door and gestured to Wade with his cane. "Let's go in the den and talk."

"I'll be right there," Wade promised, then redirected his focus to Cat. "You aren't leaving, are you?"

"I was on my way to the barn. Today's the day for our employee Christmas party."

"Oh." A frown flickered across his face.

"You're welcome to come," Cat inserted quickly, then hesitated. "That's if you can stay for it."

"I can stay," he assured her. "I was just thinking about the dinner plans we made."

Cat was so relieved, she almost laughed out loud. "No one will mind if I slip out before the party's over. Jessy and Trey are obligated to stay for the bulk of it. But Dad and I are free to leave anytime."

"Then we still have a date."

Cat allowed a wide smile to claim her mouth. "And I intend to see that you keep it."

"You aren't going to get any protest from me."
He darted a glance at the house. "I'd better not
keep Chase waiting. See you later."

As he moved around her and up the steps, Cat
remembered. "Would you mind driving Dad
down to the barn after you two finish talking?"

"Be glad to." He sketched her a wave and
slipped into the house.

In high spirits, Cat almost glided down the steps
to the car. Suddenly everything seemed
incredibly wonderful.

Chapter 9

After a search of Jake's sock drawer failed to turn up his missing sandals, Sloan rummaged through the next drawer. She struck pay dirt in the bottom and last drawer, pulling out first one sandal from beneath a stack of clean pajamas and the second one that had been tucked deep in the corner.

The sandals weren't the only items she discovered. The drawer was clearly where Jake stashed his "treasures," everything from an old chipped arrowhead to an old Hot Wheels car. Privately Sloan wondered how she had missed discovering any of it before, then acknowledged that she hadn't been looking for them—or even guessed that anything existed that Jake would feel the need to secret away. She smiled to herself, realizing she had learned another lesson in child-rearing.

With the drawer's contents straightened and his other treasures returned to their hiding places, Sloan grabbed the sandals and stood up. As she left his bedroom, she reminded herself to thank Cat for the suggestion. She didn't care to think about how much time she would have wasted searching other areas of his room before checking the chest of drawers.

She ran quickly and lightly down the steps, a smile of satisfaction curling her lips. As she swung around the newel post at the base of the staircase, she heard Chase's voice coming from the den and realized that he and Cat hadn't left for the party yet. She crossed directly to the open doorway.

"Hey, Cat, you were right." She held out the sandals in triumph and opened her mouth to say more, but the sight of Wade Rogers seated in the wingbacked chair in front of the desk stopped any more words from coming out. Feeling both men's gazes on her, Sloan forced an apologetic smile. "Sorry. I thought Cat was in here."

"No, she's already left for the barn," Chase told her.

"I'm going too." As Sloan backed out of the opening, two things registered—the ballpoint pen Chase was holding and the open checkbook beneath his hand.

There was only one conclusion she could draw from that, Chase was writing another check to Wade Rogers. For what? And how much this time?

The questions nagged Sloan all the way to the barn. Her first thought was to find Trey and let him know what she'd seen. But one look at the crowd in the barn and Sloan knew this wasn't the time or the place to talk about her suspicions. Sloan settled instead for locating her son and getting him into his costume. To do that, she had to find Jessy, who had volunteered to keep an eye on Jake while Sloan went to locate his sandals.

Scanning faces, she started working her way through the throng. A second later, she spotted Jessy and altered her course toward her mother-in-law.

"You found them!" Cat's voice came from her left.

Sloan paused to reply as Cat closed the gap between them. "In the pajama drawer. Thanks for the hint."

Cat smiled away her thanks. "Jake is his father's son."

"True." Sloan found it impossible not to notice how incredibly alive and happy Cat looked. She looked radiant and positively youthful. It didn't call for any great deal of imagination for Sloan to guess why. "I noticed that Wade made it here after all."

"I know." Cat fairly beamed. "He volunteered to bring Dad down when they were finished. Hopefully that won't be too long." Her glance strayed to the barn's entrance.

"It better not be, or Chase will miss the children's program. Which reminds me. I need to get Jake in his costume."

"Good luck," Cat said with a laugh.

On her way to Jessy, Sloan spotted Jake playing with two of his friends not far from where his grandmother stood. Jake looked anything but happy when he saw the sandals in her hand. Grudgingly he let Sloan lead him to the tack room that served as a string room for the Christmas program's props and a changing room for the children. With ill grace, he removed his cowboy hat and boots, trading them for the sandals and turbaned headdress, then donned his shepherd's robe.

Sloan all but dragged him out of the tack room. "How come I had to change now?" Jake grumbled. "It isn't even time yet. See." He pointed to his friend. "Dan doesn't have his costume on yet."

"He soon will," Sloan assured him, then noticed Chase standing next to Jessy. Wade Rogers wasn't with him. "Your Greypa's here."

Chase was quick to greet the boy. "Well, Jake, I see you're in your costume already. Good for you."

"No, it isn't," Jake declared. "My toes are cold."

An eyebrow arched in mild reproof. "I don't hear any of the other boys complaining, and you shouldn't either."

"I guess," he mumbled. He heaved a big sigh of resignation and made a big show out of lifting his downcast head. Abruptly his expression lost its disgruntled look. "Hey, Greypa, there's Aunt Cat. She's with the husband you got her." He pointed to the couple a short distance away from them.

"Now, he isn't her husband yet," Chase corrected.

"But he just put his arm around her. That means he likes her, doesn't it?"

"I'm pretty sure he likes her," Chase agreed.

"I bet it's a special kind of liking, the same as me and Becky." Jake nodded in certainty.

"Who's Becky?" Jessy wanted to know.

"A girl. She's in the play, too."

Chase exchanged an amused look with Jessy. "Really?"

"What part does she play?"

Jake thought for a second. "She's supposed to be Mary. She has really long hair and a blue dress." He looked down doubtfully at his burlap robe. "Is this a dress? It's scratchy. Aren't shepherds s'posed to wear jeans?"

"I've never seen one in jeans," Chase stated.

Sloan shook her head, confirming Chase's statement, gave the rope belt around his waist an adjusting tug. He looked up in time to see Cat smiling up at Wade, and cupping a hand over the one he had on her waist as if to keep it there.

"Aunt Cat likes him a lot, too, Greypa."

His grandfather chuckled. "Yes, she does."

"Has she started thinking it's her idea and not yours?" he wondered.

Sloan took him by the hand. "Come on," she said to Jake. "Let's go see if the other kids are ready yet."

Jake didn't protest and for once didn't drag his feet. Sloan suspected that little Becky might have something to do with that.

"Did you practice your part?" she asked as they walked to the improvised stage.

"I sure did."

He rattled off the few lines assigned to him and Sloan smiled, squeezing the warm little fingers in hers with maternal affection. "Very good. I'm proud of you."

Wade kept his arm around Cat as if it was the most natural thing in the world to do so. The occasional curious glance they got from others at the party didn't seem to faze him in the least.

"So all of these people work on the ranch?" he asked in a low voice.

"All of them. Some are married. Some aren't. Most were born and raised here."

"Really?" Wade seemed genuinely interested.

Warming to the subject, Cat nodded at a group standing around the punch bowl. "Really. Those over there are third and fourth generation on the Triple C."

"I'm impressed. They really are like family. Now I understand why you and I are being watched. Discreetly, of course."

She was pleased Wade was a quick study, but not surprised by his instinctive understanding of the relationship between the Calder clan and the people who worked for them. They really were an extended family and it was never more evident than around the holiday season.

• • •

"Need some help?" Sloan asked the woman in charge of the Christmas play. Babette Nevins was on her knees, pinning up a burlap robe for a boy who was shorter than Jake.

"You bet," the other woman replied, straightening the rough fabric. The boy took a step away from her, but she shook her head. "Not so fast, Eddy. I have to baste the hem."

Jake leaned closer to Sloan. "Baste? Isn't that what Aunt Cat does to the turkey and ham?" Jake whispered with a hint of worry.

Sloan fought back a smile and nodded. "Yes, but in this case it means something different. And she said hem, not ham. That's the bottom of the robe. It's too long. Mrs. Nevins is going to sew up the material so he doesn't trip on it."

"Oh," Jake said.

Babette took a threaded needle from a fat, tomato-shaped pincushion on the floor next to her. "Hold still," she instructed Eddy, and got to work, sticking the pins into the pincushion as she removed them.

A little girl in a flowing blue robe came over to see what was going on, clutching one hand in the folds of the same blue fabric that was draped over her head. Sloan felt Jake's grip tighten and glanced down. Jake's gaze was fixed on the girl's face.

"Hi, Becky," he said.

"Hello," she replied demurely.

"Do you want me to fasten that cloth for you?" Sloan asked her. She'd seen a safety pin among the straight pins Babette was working with.

"Yes, please." Becky let go as Sloan knelt down and safety-pinned the draped material carefully so it wouldn't slip off. Jake watched with interest. Another little girl came over, cute as could be, a curly, white, fake-fur pelt slung over her shoulders and fastened in front, clearly intended to be a sheep's costume. Black knitted gloves stood in for hooves and a black headband held sheep ears made from felt in place behind her golden braids.

"Who are you?" Sloan asked, aware that some of the ranch families had visiting relatives staying with them and the Christmas play needed plenty of young actors to fill up the improvised stage.

"I'm Lizabeth," she announced.

"Oh. What part do you play?" Sloan asked politely, even though the answer was fairly obvious.

"I'm the second sheep," the little girl replied. "I don't have to say anything."

"Yes, you do," Babette reminded her, after sticking the pins safely into the pincushion. "You get to baa, remember? Let's hear it."

Lizabeth took a deep breath and obliged with several long baas. The two boys and Becky giggled behind their hands.

"Hey," Lizabeth said indignantly. "That's what sheep sound like. My big sister raised lambs for a 4-H project, so I know."

"You're absolutely right," Sloan assured, suppressing a smile of her own. The little girl's outraged expression wasn't very sheeplike and neither were the braids.

"Hmm," Babette mused. "I think we should cut that down to one baa. Okay with you?"

Lizabeth pouted.

"Don't forget that the animals stand in back," the little girl in blue pointed out. "I'm in front. The whole time."

Her friend's pout turned into a scowl but Babette intervened before the unhappy little sheep could object to her role being shortened.

"That'll do, kids." She rolled her eyes at Sloan, as if saying "Actors and their egos." "And Becky, please remember that everyone's part is as important as yours. Now I want all of you to do a last read-through of your lines. Showtime is in fifteen minutes."

"I lost the paper," Eddy said.

"Your mom has extra copies."

He looked guilt-stricken.

"Just ask her." Babette laughed. "She won't get mad."

"Okay, Mrs. Nevins," he answered respectfully.

Becky smoothed her blue robe and walked away, followed by Lizabeth, who threw a dark look over her shoulder at the two boys. There could be trouble in Bethlehem tonight, Sloan thought, tickled by the pint-size rivalries.

She got the extra copies of the two-page play and helped Babette herd the children into a quieter area. An older kid, a gawky thirteen-year-old who hadn't taken out the earbuds in his ears, was listening to music while he rolled and unrolled a scroll on a spindle.

"Who's that boy?" she asked.

"That's Dave," Babette said. "He's our last-minute replacement for the angel. Actually, he's a blessing in disguise. The wings came out longer than we expected and he's tall enough that they don't drag the floor."

Sloan glanced at the swooping, feather-bedecked cardboard shapes attached to the back of the full-sleeved robe the teenager wore. The wings' tips cleared the floor by a foot. "So far, so good," she murmured. "What happened to the first angel?"

"He came down with a stuffy nose and sore throat. Are you ready, Dave?" she asked the tall boy.

Dave looked startled but he unrolled the scroll with a flourish and cleared his throat before he pretended to read from it. "Wow! Listen up, people! I bring you tidings of great joy! Awesome!" he said loudly.

"That's not what it says on the scroll," Babette said dryly. "Take out the ear things so you can hear me, okay? The first word is 'behold,' not 'wow.' And you can drop the second line and the 'awesome' while you're at it."

He got it right the next time. The other kids did fine, remembering nearly all of what they were supposed to say.

"Very good," Babette told them. She turned to Sloan. "We'd better do this for real before they forget," she whispered. Both women guided the group of children to the stage platform, and had them wait at one side.

Sloan went up the wooden stairs and pulled together the makeshift stage curtains. Then she motioned to Babette to bring the children onto the stage.

Beyond the curtains everyone began drifting over, chatting with each other, but watching the curtains, waiting for the moment when they would open. There was an occasional bump from a child walking behind them but no little faces to be seen.

Among the onlookers, many stood, but some found folding chairs to sit on, creating a couple of irregular rows. Chase was in front, dead center, seated on a wooden armchair that befitted a family patriarch. He waited for the play to begin, a composed expression on his weathered face. He accepted a printed program from the Martin girl, who had a basket of them on her arm, and nodded his thanks.

"He must have seen this dozens of times," Wade murmured, standing well in the back with Cat.

"Scores," Cat agreed. "But look at the twinkle in his eye. He enjoys it as much as all the other parents."

They joined the enthusiastic applause that greeted the two small shepherds who clutched the edges of the curtains and ran to either side to reveal the stage.

The costumed children were positioned in a nativity scene, looking out at their audience with a mixture of expressions, from calm to jittery.

Babette read the opening narration and stepped aside to let the play begin. Dave came forward, unrolled his scroll, and announced the impending birth of Jesus to the shepherds watching by night.

When he finished, Jake confronted him. "Next time, ask God to have Jesus borned in Montana so I can wear my boots," he blurted out.

The crowd erupted in laughter, even Chase. When the happy noise dwindled down, the play continued without a hitch. The children hit their marks and remembered their lines, telling the old, old story of the night in Bethlehem with no more ad-libs or flubs. The great star, which looked suspiciously like a pierced tin pie-plate, blazed against the dark backdrop and Becky gazed tenderly into the straw-filled basket that cradled the unseen Christ Child.

There was a brief rustle of programs as the audience joined the children in singing "Silent Night." As soon as the last note died away, the applause began and the young actors ran forward to take their bows, some proud, some self-conscious, but all pleased with themselves.

"That went well," Babette said to Sloan. "Jake was the hit of the show, though."

"He certainly got a laugh," she answered with a wry smile.

"Arms up," Babette ordered the kids waiting in line when they left the stage. She shucked the costumes over their heads with practiced speed and handed them to Sloan to fold and put into a big cardboard box. The children ran back to claim the praise from their parents. Dave didn't bother to change and walked away in his angel's costume, rocking to the music coming into his earbuds. Evidently wings were cool, Sloan decided.

As expected, Sloan found Jake half-draped across the arm of Chase's chair, chattering away, dividing his attention between Chase and Jessy. While Sloan had been helping Babette, Jake had run back to the tack room and retrieved his boots.

The instant Jake saw her, he ran to meet her. "Greypa said the program was the bestest he ever seen."

"I hope you thanked him for that."

Nodding, Jake made an agreeing sound. "And Grandma said I did my lines perfect."

"And what did she think of your ad-lib?" Sloan asked in a mildly teasing voice.

Jake screwed up his face in a puzzled frown. "What's that?"

"Nothing." She laughed and gave the brim of his cowboy hat a playful, downward tap. "Have you seen your dad?"

"He was here at first. He had to leave, though," Jake explained. "He said he had something important to do, but he'd be back."

"If he said he'll be back, then he will," Sloan declared, fully aware of where her husband had gone and why.

Jake caught hold of her hand and pulled her over to Chase's chair. "I told Mom that you thought I did good."

Suppressing a smile, Jessy asked, "And did you tell her what part you want to play in next year's program?"

"I forgot," he said in self-disgust then turned an earnest look on Sloan. "Next year I want to be the angel."

Surprised by his choice, Sloan decided the wings were even cooler than she realized. "Why the angel?"

He propped one hand on his hip in a slightly challenging pose. "'Cause that boy got to wear his boots."

Try as she might, Sloan couldn't choke off the laugh that bubbled from her. Chase and Jessy chuckled along with her.

"You can take a lot of things away from a cowboy, but don't touch his boots," Chase declared.

"At least, not this cowboy's," Sloan agreed and gave his hat another downward tug.

"Quit, Mom."

At that moment, Jake's best friend Dan came running up and grabbed his arm. "Come on, Jake. Hurry. Santa's here."

Turning in place, Sloan spotted the tall figure dressed in the traditional stocking cap and red Santa suit, sporting a long white beard and toting a sack bulging with presents, making his way to the stage area, already surrounded by children. The costume fooled the children, but Sloan recognized Trey's dark eyes and rugged features despite the masking beard.

He winked at her as he passed. When he reached the stage, he slid the big sack off his shoulder, placed both hands on his stomach and issued a hearty "Ho! Ho! Ho!", then attempted to discreetly pull strands of fake beard out of his mouth. Sloan had to laugh. Automatically she glanced to see where Jake was.

The minute she noticed him staring with fierce intensity at Santa Claus, she knew the jig was up. "Oh-oh," she murmured and hurried forward, practically pushing her way to Jake's side.

She arrived just as he thrust out an accusing finger. "Hey, how come—"

She clamped a silencing hand over his mouth and steered him out of the group of children. Only when she judged they were a safe distance away did Sloan remove her hand from his mouth and kneel down in front of him.

"That was Dad. How come he's wearing Santa's clothes?" Jake demanded.

"Santa had to be somewhere else tonight, and because he knew how disappointed all the children would be, he asked your dad to pretend to be him just for tonight," Sloan explained. "And Santa asked him to keep it a secret. So don't you tell the other kids. Okay?"

"If it's a secret, how come you know?"

For a split second she wasn't sure how to answer that. "Mothers always know everything."

He sighed a big sigh. "Like where my sandals were."

"Exactly." She almost hugged him for that. "Now, Santa left a present for you, so you go get it. But remember—not a word to the others. Promise?"

"I promise." He nodded. Then his expression turned a little smug that he knew something his friends didn't.

Releasing him, Sloan straightened and watched as Jake ran back to the stage area, all smiles. Jessy came up on her left and exchanged a knowing glance with her.

"He recognized Trey, didn't he?" she guessed.

"You saw that, too," Sloan realized.

"It was obvious. To everybody," she added. "I'm not surprised. It's hard to fool a Calder."

Sloan immediately thought of Wade Rogers, and remembered Trey's utter lack of suspicion about the man. She felt a little guilty for not fully sharing his opinion. Blind trust had never been something Sloan found easy to give.

Without thinking, she skimmed the crowd, looking for Cat and Wade. Almost immediately she made eye contact with Cat, who waved, then signaled that she and Wade were leaving. Sloan acknowledged the message with a high lift of her head and waved back, then nudged Jessy.

"Cat and Wade are off to dinner." She nodded in the direction of the departing couple.

"Good. I was hoping Cat wouldn't feel under any obligation to do more than put in an appearance here."

"Do you think Wade is the right man for her?" Sloan couldn't help wondering about that.

"It doesn't matter what I think. Her feelings are the only ones that count," Jessy replied in a calm, steady voice that fully accepted whatever decision Cat made.

Chapter 10

Forty-five minutes after leaving Triple C headquarters, Cat and Wade pulled up to the east gate. "Which way?" Wade asked, glancing at her while keeping one hand on the steering wheel.

"Blue Moon is to the north," Cat pointed left.

The headlights sent long beams of white over the winter landscape as the rented SUV made the turn and took aim on the Big Dipper.

Being alone with him was something Cat welcomed, although she still found herself searching for what to say. Wade kept the conversation neutral, and she was grateful for that, answering his questions about the area as they drove into the night.

"How far is it to town?" he wanted to know, adding, "I mean in minutes. The distances out here in Montana are mind-boggling."

"Oh, we don't even notice the miles." Cat laughed. "It's about fifteen or twenty minutes. I'm not sure you would even call it a town."

"Typical wide spot in the road, huh?"

"Definitely."

Wade smiled and leaned back a little as he drove. A semi was ahead of them, but it quickly disappeared. "Looks like we have the highway to ourselves."

"There hasn't been much traffic since Dy-Corp

closed its coal-mining operation," Cat admitted. "And once again, the population of Blue Moon dropped to just a few when the workers moved somewhere else to make a living."

"Once again." Wade picked up on the phrase she had used. "You mean it's happened before."

"Back during the drought and depression years. Instead of coal being the cause of the town's boom, it was the immigrants who flooded in, took out homesteads and tried to grow wheat. When the rains didn't come and the wells dried up, they watched their land blow away along with their dreams."

"And they had to leave, too," he guessed.

"All except my grandmother, who wisely stayed and married my grandfather," Cat added lightly.

"She was wise indeed," Wade agreed and cast a curious sideways glance at Cat. "What was she like?"

"I don't know. I never knew her. She died shortly after my father was born." Cat thought of something else that he might find interesting. "I forgot to tell you how Blue Moon got its name— at least, according to local legend. Supposedly a trader called Fat Frank Fitzsimmons was traveling the area with a wagonload of supplies and whiskey. His wagon broke down where the town now stands. Unable to fix it, he set up shop and nailed up a sign that said WHISKEY. Few days later a cowboy rode by, saw it and stopped for some of that whiskey. It seems he warned Fat Frank that he was doomed because folks only came this way once in a blue moon. After the cowboy left, Frank wrote under his whiskey sign, Blue Moon, Montana Territory. And that's how it got its start and a name."

Wade chuckled softly. "Whether it's true or not, it's definitely colorful. And this place where we're going, is that where Fat Frank sold his whiskey?"

"No, the Feddersons bought his place and ran a general store there for years. Then they sold it to the Kellys, who basically turned it into a large convenience store and gas station. The place we're going got its start as a roadhouse during the prohibition years. After all, Canada isn't that far away," she reminded him. "I've heard the old-timers whisper that the proprietor had some very attractive 'nieces' who worked there."

"Sin always sells, doesn't it?"

"So I've heard." Cat smiled. "Ross and Marsha Kelly own it now. It's right up there—Kelly's Bar and Grill." She pointed to the building's sign. "It's a much more respectable place now, I'm glad to say."

Wade slowed and made the turn into the parking lot of Kelly's. Cat released her seat belt when the car stopped and got out without waiting for him to come around and open her door. The brisk night air felt invigorating, increasing her sense of being fully alive.

He didn't bother to button up for the short walk to the door and neither did she. He took her arm in his and she accepted the courteous gesture without a moment's hesitation. The strength and warmth of his light hold felt very right and natural.

"Busier than I expected," Wade commented as they headed for a table. The walls were decorated with paper Christmas motifs and the windows had been looped with strings of colored lights, the old-fashioned big ones.

She nodded. "But not exactly packed like a typical Saturday night," Cat replied, her glance making its own sweep of the place. There were only two or three couples dancing to music from the jukebox. She recognized the song, a hit from a while ago that had never lost its popularity. Her gaze moved to the back and stayed on the rectangle of green felt under a spotlight and the random arrangement of colorful billiard balls on it. An ancient cowboy was bent over the table, playing pool with some much younger ranch hands, who stood to the side with long cues in hand. One was busily twirling a small cube of blue chalk on the tip of his cue just for something to do. But there wasn't the usual number of onlookers.

The sharp click of billiard balls got Wade's

attention. Ricocheting off two others in turn, a striper rolled straight and true, and dropped into a far pocket with a solid thunk. The watching men scowled. Wade paused for a fraction of a second to watch the old man line up another complex shot. He sank the next ball he'd indicated with practiced smoothness.

"He knows what he's doing," he said with a low chuckle. "The competition doesn't look too happy."

Cat smiled in silent agreement. The ancient cowboy straightened as they passed by several feet away and took a moment to tip his hat to her, a faint but wily smile of triumph on his wrinkled face as he nodded to both of them.

They responded in kind and picked a table with an extra seat for their coats, sitting down. Marsha bustled over. "Evenin', you two. Kind of a surprise to see you here, Cat, what with the ranch party going on tonight."

"We snuck away," Cat told her and touched a forefinger to her lips. "Don't tell anyone."

An answering smile increased her apple-cheeked look as Marsha winked and promised, "Mum's the word. Now what can I get for you?"

Wade ordered a beer and Cat asked for a Coke.

"Nachos to start?" Marsha suggested.

Wade folded his arms on the table and grinned up at Marsha. "I try to say yes to temptation. If you're talking nachos, the answer is hell yes."

"What kind of dip? We have salsa or cheese."

"Both," Cat said impulsively.

"You've got it." Marsha departed for the bar.

His grin softened to a smile when he looked across the table at her. "Both, huh? You're my kind of girl, Cat."

"That's nice to know," she said, pleased by the frank tenderness in his casual remark. A playful part of her couldn't resist adding a teasing, "At least I think it is."

"It is." Wade reached out a hand and brushed her cheek with the back of his knuckles. The brief touch wasn't that intimate, but it seared her. Cat sensed he was aware of her reaction to it. "Was that over the line for such a public place?"

"Not really," she said, lifting her head to a proud tilt.

"Sorry." He looked into her eyes as if he was gauging her mood.

Cat willed her racing pulse to slow down. "Don't be. I truly didn't mind."

The drinks and nachos were coming their way on the tray that Marsha held in one hand as she wove between the tables. "Here ya go." She set down coasters printed with four-leaf clovers and positioned the beer and soda on them, popping in two straws, added the rest of their order and left in a hurry. A few more customers had arrived.

Cat removed the paper from her straw and took a long sip of icy, refreshing Coke, looking up at

Wade, who was turning the nacho plate around to study the cheese-drenched chips. "Yes indeed. They look good and greasy. Dibs on the big ones," he said. "I might let you have a few, though."

Cat laughed. "How do you stay in such good shape?"

"I run. Play tennis. Ski. Basically, if it involves moving, I'm your man."

"I'm glad to hear it."

"And you?"

Cat picked up a nacho and nibbled on the corner. "Living on a ranch automatically means being active. I ride a lot. Swim in the summer, fish a little. And I'm always walking."

He nodded to the dancers, who were stepping to a lively tune. "How about that?"

"Sure. Uh—sometimes. I used to love to go dancing."

He caught the wistful note in her voice and asked gently, "How long has it been since you did?"

Cat didn't answer right away. "I don't know," she said finally.

Wade took a healthy swallow of beer and set down the frosty mug. "After dinner, we can take a turn on the floor if you like."

She nodded. "I'd enjoy that."

"So how long have you lived on the Triple C?" he asked.

"Almost all my life," she replied, "minus the time I spent at college." Cat paused a beat, then added, "I'm including the years Logan and I lived on the Circle Six ranch. It borders the Triple C so it hardly seems to count as living somewhere else."

"Ever think of moving?"

The question surprised her. "Where?"

"It doesn't matter. I was just curious."

She shook her head very slightly. "Moving isn't something that's occurred to me. No, that's not completely true," Cat corrected. "Since my son Quint took over running the C Bar ranch in Texas, I have toyed with the idea of moving there, so I can see my young grandson a little more often."

"You have a grandson?" he said.

"His name's Josh. He will be two years old soon. All three of them will be flying up for Christmas in a few days, so I'll get to see him then."

"You Calders are a close-knit clan," Wade observed.

Cat acknowledged that immutable truth with a rueful nod and smiled. "You know what they say about the ties that bind. Family ties are strongest."

"And they last the longest, it seems." Wade was thoughtful. "Chase filled me in on some of the family history. He even showed me that old map of the ranch, which got him started talking about the first cattle drives from Texas to Montana. Fascinating story. More like a saga, really."

"It must sound like that," Cat admitted and let her gaze wander over his face. In the dim light of the dining area, he was even more attractive than usual. The touch of silver in his hair suited him, and the sexy twinkle in his eye when he looked at her was making her feel very special.

Marsha stopped by their table again. "Is everything all right? Did you want to order dinner yet?"

"I think I'd better look at the menu first." Wade removed two from their table holder and passed one of them to Cat.

"Take your time. Don't let me rush you," Marsha told them. "Whenever you're ready to order, just flag me down."

"Will do," Cat promised and went through the motion of glancing at the menu choices even though she already knew what she would find. "Anything you would recommend?"

"Well, they serve Calder beef, so the steaks here are excellent."

"Naturally." Wade grinned.

The old barn with its massive timbers was alive with laughter and chattering voices. This was the strictly social time that all the ranch families looked forward to, coming after the children's program, Santa's visit, and the assault on the long

200

buffet tables that had been laden with platters and bowls of food. A few continued to graze on the pickings that remained at the buffet, something that was likely to go on the rest of the night. The remnants of a piñata, a Texas tradition that had traveled north to Montana along with the Longhorns, still hung from a low rafter, its contents long ago spilled to the delight of the children.

For most, this was the shank of the evening with a lot of partying yet to be done and stories to be swapped. Only the very young showed any signs of tiring. And one in particular, Sloan noted, spotting her son sitting Indian-fashion on the floor next to Chase's chair, seemingly content merely to watch the goings-on rather than tear around with his friends like a hooligan. Sloan observed the way he was leaning against the chair leg.

She nudged a shoulder against Trey and nodded in Jake's direction. "I think it's a certain little boy's bedtime."

Trey glanced his son's way just as Jake let his head loll back against the chair. "Give him another minute and he'll be asleep."

"It's a thought. Except he's twice as heavy to carry when he's asleep. I'd better go put him to bed," Sloan decided and started forward.

"Tell him I'll be up directly to tuck him in."

Sloan responded with an acknowledging wave and made her way to Chase's chair. His head was bent toward Stumpy Niles as if to better hear what Stumpy was saying. Chase gave her a questioning look when she paused in front of his chair.

"I decided it was time to claim this sleepy boy at your feet," she told him and bent down to pick up Jake.

"Are you taking him up to the house?" Chase asked.

Sloan nodded and shifted the boy in her arms so more of his weight rode on her hip. "It's time he was in bed."

Her statement roused a protest from Jake. "I'm not tired, Mom."

"Just the same, you're going to bed."

"Aww, I don't want to." His head dipped onto her shoulder, belying his words.

"Mind if I ride along with you?" Chase asked, gripping his cane and preparing to stand. "It's time I called it a night, too."

"Of course you can ride with us. Can't he, Jake?" She looked down at her son, who managed a tired nod, then stood back to wait for Chase.

Stumpy Niles stood up when Chase did. "I guess I'll try to find the old lady. We need to be headin' home, too. Good visitin' with you, Chase."

"Same here," Chase replied and struck out for the exit, not seeming to notice how readily a path was made for him.

Outside, Sloan settled Jake in his car seat, then slid behind the wheel. As she reached to pull the door shut, she glanced to make sure Chase was safely in. With the brightness of the overhead light fully illuminating his craggy features, she noticed for the first time how haggard and worn-out he looked. The discovery brought a sudden attack of conscience.

"I'm sorry, Chase. I should have checked to see if you wanted to leave earlier." She had grown too used to Cat being the one who kept an eye on him.

"No problem. In fact it was a bit of welcome change not to have Cat worrying over me all evening." When Sloan started to speak, Chase waved off her words. "I know. She means well."

Sloan chose to lightly chide him. "A man who doesn't mind a woman fussing over him? Now that is a surprise."

Chase grunted an amused response, then said in all seriousness, "She has too many good years left to waste them on me."

"I'm sure Cat doesn't think they're wasted."

Chase made no reply to that. In fact he said nothing more during the short drive from the barn to the Homestead. He was already at the front steps by the time Sloan had gotten Jake out of the car seat. She hurried to catch up with him, then held the door for him.

She hesitated in the foyer and cast an uncertain

glance at him when he stopped to shrug out of his coat. "Is there anything I can get you before I take Jake upstairs?"

"No. In fact I'm heading straight to bed myself." He lifted his coat onto a hook, then collected the cane he had propped against the wall. "See you in the morning, Jake."

"See ya," Jake mumbled.

Sloan deliberately took her time crossing to the oak staircase, her ears tuned to the sounds of Chase's cane as he made his way to his bedroom in the west wing. The rhythm remained steady, assuring her that he needed no assistance from her.

In the bedroom, Jake stirred sufficiently to give her some help changing out of his clothes and into his pajamas. He sat motionless on the edge of the bed while she pulled back the covers. Rather clumsily Jake rolled over and slid under the sheets.

"Isn't Dad coming?" he asked in a halfhearted attempt to stave off the inevitable. "Maybe I should wait."

"I don't think he'll mind if I tuck you in instead of him," Sloan assured him. "He'll be up to tell you good night though. Would you like me to read you a story while we wait for him?"

"Yeah." He nodded, then abruptly threw the covers back. "I forgot to say my prayers."

"While you do that, I'll get your book."

Sloan walked over to the bookshelf and selected his favorite story, smiling to herself while she listened to the familiar—and somehow comfortable—words of his prayer. "Now I lay me down to sleep." He finished by asking blessings for each member of the family, said his "Amen" and started to rise, then knelt hastily again. "I forgot. God, please don't let Josh break any of my toys when he comes. Amen." After he crawled back under the covers, he gave her a worried, "It's alright to ask God for that, isn't it?"

"I'm sure He won't mind." Sloan sat on the edge of the bed and opened the storybook.

As she expected, his eyes drifted shut before she was halfway through it. When she closed the book on the last page, Jake was sound asleep. She adjusted the covers around his slender body and lightly kissed the top of his head, whispering a "Good night, sweetie." A term he would have been horrified by if he was awake to hear it.

Sloan made a noiseless retreat from the room, switched off the light, leaving only the soft glow of a night-light in the room, and pulled the door partway shut.

The stillness of the Homestead moved over her as she descended the staircase. The easy quiet was a welcome change after the hubbub of the barn. With Chase in the house, Sloan knew she was free to return to the barn, but she decided to wait for Trey.

She was halfway into the living room when her glance strayed to the doorway of the darkened den. She stopped, remembering the glimpse she'd had of the open checkbook and Chase's hand poised over it, and Wade seated by the desk. All those unanswered questions came rushing back. Sloan tried to convince herself none of it was any of her business. But curiosity got the better of her.

She crossed to the den, started to flip on the light, then darted a guilty look in the direction of Chase's bedroom. The hall was dark, no sliver of light showing beneath his door. Before she got cold feet, she hit the switch, flooding the room with light.

At the desk, she opened two drawers before she found the one that contained his checkbook. She laid it on the desk and flipped through the stubs to the last page.

Just as she suspected, the last check had been made payable to Wade Rogers. Her fingertip slid across the stub and came to a stop on the amount.

One hundred thousand dollars.

Numb with shock, Sloan could only stare at the number, unable to believe what she was seeing. Her thoughts raced, searching for some reason that might justify it. She never heard the front door open—or the approach of footsteps. She didn't know Trey was in the house until he spoke from the doorway.

"What are you doing in here, Sloan?"

She looked up in surprise, but the guilt she might have felt earlier at being caught snooping was completely overwhelmed by her discovery.

"You need to see this, Trey," she insisted.

"See what?" His gaze narrowed, sharp with disapproval and challenge.

Belatedly she registered the displeasure in his expression, and the veiled accusation in his look. She didn't flinch from either. "Earlier today your grandfather wrote a check to Wade Rogers in the amount of one hundred thousand dollars." She enunciated the number with slow emphasis.

As much as Trey tried to conceal it, Sloan could tell that he was taken aback by the size of the figure.

Almost hesitant, he walked over to the desk and looked at the stub for himself. He didn't immediately say anything. Sloan filled the silence instead.

"The other check he gave Wade, it seemed logical to think it was a donation. Even a political contribution. But a hundred thousand dollars, Trey. That's an alarming amount. Even you must realize that."

"It does raise questions." But Trey's admission was a grudging one. "It still doesn't change the fact that the check was drawn on Chase's personal account. He doesn't have to answer to me—or anyone else—about how he chooses to spend his money."

Unable to argue with that, Sloan said, "I'm just thinking about the stories you hear of the elderly being targeted by scam artists."

"You think Rogers is a scam artist?" Trey seemed more amused by the possibility than suspicious.

"We don't really know anything except what we've been told—either by Chase or Wade himself. I think we should check into his background. Make sure he is who he claims to be."

Trey dismissed the suggestion with a negative shake of his head. "Old and occasionally forgetful, Gramps might be, but he's still sharp enough to see through any confidence trick." He closed the checkbook with a decisive firmness. "Right now we're going to put this away and forget we ever saw that stub."

Sloan looked at him aghast. "How can we?"

He returned the checkbook to its drawer, then lightly gripped her shoulders and squared her around to face him. "When I first saw you in here, I was more than a little angry that you'd been snooping. Then I realized you did it out of genuine concern. That makes me proud you care that much. It's one more thing I love about you."

As pleased as Sloan was to know that he understood her motives, she knew when she was being manipulated. "You're trying to change the subject."

"I almost succeeded." A smile played at the corners of his mouth. "I know, come Monday morning, you're going to be tempted to call one of your lawyers and have them run a background check on Rogers. I want you to give me your word that you won't do that. At least, not yet."

"But, Trey—" she began in protest.

"There could be a very legitimate reason for a check this size," he reasoned. "For now, I just want to watch and wait. Agree?"

Sloan hesitated, then realized much of his reluctance stemmed from his refusal to believe that age had in any way diminished his grandfather's abilities. His whole life he had looked up to Chase. Trey couldn't bring himself to think that he might have become any less of a man—and definitely without more evidence.

"I agree," Sloan promised. "I won't do or say anything unless something else happens."

"It won't." He slid an arm around her shoulders and gathered her to his side. "Let's go upstairs and check on that son of ours."

Chapter 11

After Marsha Kelly cleared away their dinner plates, Wade glanced across the table at Cat. "You were right. The steak was delicious."

"So was mine, though there was more of it than I could eat."

"Blame it on the nachos," he told her, then glanced toward the small dance floor near the bar area where a couple was doing a spirited two step. They ended the song with a flourish.

"They were good," Wade observed, and added ruefully, "I don't think I could do it that well."

Cat laughed softly. "You don't have to be perfect. Just follow the music."

He chuckled. "And you follow me?"

"Something like that."

He got up and extended a hand to her. "Then may I have this dance?"

"Yes." She rose from her chair, feeling as giddy as if she'd been drinking champagne and not a plain old Coke.

Wade warmly clasped the hand she placed in his, leading her to the dance floor without another word. There were three couples on it now, moving through the last steps of a cowboy waltz. The jukebox, a vintage machine with actual records, made faint mechanical noises as the song that was playing ended and another began.

"Uh-oh." He laughed. "Is that swing or polka?"

"I'm not sure. We can improvise." She didn't care what the music was. Being in his arms felt wonderful. "I think a polka is a half skip and then a slide," she murmured. "But whatever you do, keep moving."

He took a deep breath and clasped her waist, lifting her hand high with his as he whirled her across the floor. She was breathless with the rush of moving to the exhilarating melody, laughing as she looked up at him.

Wade grinned, concentrating on leading her and not crashing into anyone else. From what she could see, none of the other couples seemed exactly expert either but they were doing their best. A few yips and hollers punctuated the music as the tune ended.

One couple left the floor for their table and the lights dimmed a bit as the next record came on. Mercifully slow, the first notes of a romantic song drifted out.

"That's more like it," Wade said softly. "Put your head on my shoulder."

She did. And she closed her eyes. If it turned out that all she would have was one night with him, being held like this was something she would always remember.

Keeping her close, moving easily, he danced with her as if he had always known her. Cat relaxed in his embrace, pliant and yielding, pleasurably aware of Wade's supple strength. Despite his initial demurrals, his lead was so natural that following him was effortless.

Dreamily, she lifted her head to look up at him and her breath caught when she saw the tenderness in his eyes. Her lips parted in surprise and he took his chance. Wade's mouth claimed hers for only a few seconds, but she found the discreet pressure of his lips overwhelmingly sensual.

With a little gasp, she broke the kiss and glanced around. No one had noticed. The only other couple left on the floor were lost in their own romantic world too.

Cat put her head back on his shoulder to hide her excited confusion. Wade made no protest, only rested his chin on the top of her hair, moving her through the last steps and final notes of a song she had never heard before but was never going to forget.

It ended.

"Shall we sit down?" he said softly.

Reluctantly, Cat gave a slight nod, brushing her cheek against the fine material of his shirt, breathing in a faint but intoxicating fragrance that was a mix of warm man and good soap.

She moved apart from him with a sigh, holding onto his hand but not daring to look into his eyes until her heart stopped racing. The intimate dance had dissolved her last shreds of reserve. It would be easy to make a fool of herself over someone like Wade Rogers. And so enjoyable.

A neon-rimmed clock on the wall caught his eye. "Hell. It's almost ten-fifteen," he muttered. He didn't sit down when they reached their table, but turned to her. "Cat, as much as I don't want the evening to end, I do have to catch a very early flight in the morning. I need to get you back to the ranch right about now."

"Oh. Are you—staying at a hotel in Miles City tonight?" Disappointment washed over her. She tried not to show it.

"I checked in before I drove to the ranch," Wade told her.

Cat picked up her purse. Marsha had already cleared away their glasses and plates. Wade opened his wallet and tossed down two bills that more than covered their tab. "Ready to go?" he asked.

"As soon as I get my coat." She kept her tone light.

The drive back to the Triple C seemed painfully short to Cat. When they arrived at the ranch headquarters, they saw plenty of vehicles parked at the old barn, indicating the party was still in full swing. An old hay-wagon, mounded with loose straw, rolled past them, drawn by a shaggy-coated team of draft horses. Several couples were snuggled together in the straw pile, mindless of the night air's chill.

"A hayride," Wade said with amusement. "Looks like fun. I wish we had more time."

We. The single word made Cat feel wistful and already alone. He drove closer to the house and parked, getting out and coming around to her side of the car to assist her.

Without saying a word, he walked her up the steps to the front door. The porch light was awfully bright after the comforting darkness of his rented car. When she looked up, his gaze locked with hers. She desperately wanted what she saw in their depths—a steady fire that hinted at strong emotion. He took her arm and drew her aside into the shadows, cupping one strong hand to her cheek and bending down to kiss her.

She wanted that even more. His lips were firm and the searching tenderness of his tongue stirred her. Wade sighed when he stopped, sliding his hand around her neck in a sensual caress. "That was our second kiss."

"Do we have to count them?" she murmured.

"No." He gazed down at her. "I was just thinking that a first kiss can be so awkward." Ever so briefly, he touched his lips to hers before she could say anything. "But ours wasn't."

She drew in a ragged breath, not able to reply.

"If you don't mind my saying so, I suspect it's been a while for you. Like dancing. Am I right?"

"Yes," she whispered.

He drew her into an open embrace. "I have to tell you something. I'm honored that I got that chance. You really are a beautiful woman, Cat."

"You certainly make me feel like one," she admitted.

"I'm coming back," he said softly. "I should make it before Christmas."

"That's not far away."

"No, it isn't," Wade replied. "As long as I don't get tripped up by delays or unforeseen problems, it should be doable."

Trembling under her warm coat, Cat tipped up her face to his, knowing what they both wanted. His last kiss was passionate.

Again, he was the one who broke it off, stroking her cheek in a final caress. "Wait for me," he said.

Cat nodded and watched him go.

The Sunday morning sunlight blazed through the windows, but there wasn't much warmth in it. The others were in the dining room when Cat made a belated entrance, attempting to be invisible. But Trey looked up.

"Morning, Aunt Cat," he said cheerfully and pushed a platter of eggs and sausage over to her when she sat down. "Everything's still hot, including the coffee."

She smiled at him. "Thanks, but I'll just have some toast, I think."

Trey passed that plate too. "Here you go."

Cat selected a slice and buttered it, nibbling a corner as she looked around at the extended family. Her father was at the head of the table, studying the commodities reports in Friday's newspapers, his half-glasses way down on his nose. The local and national newspapers got to the ranch a day or so late as a rule, but that didn't bother him. He'd finished his breakfast and had one hand curved around a refill of coffee.

Trey leaned back in his chair, in no hurry to leave. He draped an arm over the back of his wife's chair and lightly rubbed the nape of Sloan's neck, easing a hand under the high, draped collar of her hand-knit sweater to do it.

Seeing the ease and familiarity of his idle caress, Cat felt a pang of loneliness. Wade was right. It had been too long.

Briskly, she poured herself a half-cup of coffee and ate the last few bites of her toast. Jessy entered at that moment with a fresh pot in hand. "Oh—hello, Cat. I thought that one was nearly empty. Here's more if you need it." She set the second carafe down.

"Thanks. I do," Cat said.

Jessy settled into a chair opposite her and tackled a slice of toast herself before she spoke again. "So," she said, "did you and Wade enjoy yourselves last night?"

"Yes, we went to Blue Moon and had dinner at

Kelly's. We did stay at the party long enough to see the Christmas program," Cat replied. "I thought the kids did a wonderful job."

Jake piped up, "Did you see me, Aunt Cat?"

"I certainly did. And I thought your performance was excellent." She laughed.

"Thanks." He beamed at the praise.

"Did Wade mention anything about when he might be able to come back?" Jessy asked, returning to the previous subject.

Cat knew that dodging questions would only lead to more questions. "He hopes to make it before Christmas," she admitted.

Sloan's head snapped up. "So soon," she blurted, then darted a quick glance at Trey.

He acted as if he hadn't heard either of their comments. "Did you still need me to give you a hand to bring those quilts down?"

"What quilts?" Jessy asked curiously.

Accepting Trey's deft change of subject, knowing that he didn't want any of her suspicions about Wade to become known, Sloan explained, "I found a motherlode of handmade quilts in an attic closet the other day. There was a dresser blocking it. When I moved it, there they were. Some signed and dated in embroidery thread. The oldest was from 1910 and the newest is from 1939."

"I think I know the ones you mean," Jessy said slowly. "They were all made here."

Trey intervened. "Not a problem. They're in our bedroom right now and they could use a good airing."

"We could string clotheslines in the laundry room for that," Cat suggested. "And with those bright overheads, we could see if they need mending. They must after all that time in the attic."

"I thought they'd make an ideal backdrop for a family picture. I'd like to photograph all of us in front of them, especially the kids."

"That's a great idea, Sloan," Cat said.

"I thought so," Sloan replied. "Come on, Trey. Let's go get them."

"I can help," Jake declared and scrambled off his chair to hurry after them.

"Have you heard from Laredo lately?" Jessy directed her question at Chase and took a sip of coffee.

"Not for a couple days." Chase tipped his head down to peer at Jessy over his half-rimmed glasses. "Why?"

"Just curious." She shrugged, then admitted, "He hasn't called me, and every time I try his cell phone, it goes straight to voice mail."

"Feeling a little neglected, are you?" Chase observed in half jest, then shook out the folds of his paper again. "I promise he hasn't forgotten you."

"I never thought that for one minute, and you know it," she retorted.

"He's probably ignoring your messages so he doesn't accidentally let it slip where he is or what he's doing," Chase told her. "Christmas is just around the corner, you know."

"Speaking of Christmas." Jessy downed a final swallow of coffee and pushed her chair back from the table. "That reminds me I have a couple presents upstairs that need to be wrapped before it's time to get ready for church."

Halfway up the stairs, she met Trey and Sloan on their way down, each carrying a large armload of old quilts. Jessy pressed close to the railing so they would have enough room to pass. The folded fabric brushed her arm as they moved by single file, the contact unleashing that musty, dusty smell of something that had been stored away for years.

"Whew!" She waved a hand in front of her nose, trying to dispel the strong odor. "Those need a good airing."

"Tell me about it," Trey muttered in absolute agreement. "We'd better put them in the living room," he told Sloan. "We don't want to ruin somebody's breakfast."

Trey dumped his armful on the sofa cushions and left the task of separating them to Sloan. Cat came to give her a hand. She held up the first one and studied its intricate stitching.

"I'm so glad you found these, Sloan," she murmured. "It makes me wonder what else is stashed up there that we've forgotten all about."

Sloan shook out another quilt, then nodded to the one Cat held. "Did you see? That one is signed and dated."

"Millicent Clyde, December 1931," Cat read. "Finished in winter obviously, when she was housebound."

Sloan traced a finger over the embroidered name. "So long ago. Would your dad have known who she was?"

"Maybe," Cat replied. "Judy Niles certainly would've known."

Sloan nodded thoughtfully. "I think Millicent would be happy to know that her handiwork has lasted this long."

"Back then, everything had to," Cat said and quoted the old saying, "'Use it up, wear it out. Make it last or do without.' Being a ranch hand's wife wasn't the easiest life back in the day."

The thumping of a cane announced Chase's arrival. "What are you two doing?" Entering the room, Chase shot a glance at the stack of quilts and the unfolded patchwork. "Oh. Those quilts." He came over for a closer look.

"See any of your shirts here, Chase?" Sloan said in a lightly teasing voice and held out a quilt for his inspection.

He looked at the date she showed him. "No.

And my shirts aren't that old," he said gruffly.

"I'm not so sure." Cat laughed. "You've never put one in the ragbag for as long as I've known you."

"Why would I? Takes time to break in a shirt just right."

"Of course," Cat said in dry disbelief.

"Do you recognize the woman's name?" Sloan wondered.

Chase peered at the embroidery and shook his head. "No, but a lot of people lived on the Triple C over the years." Sloan began folding the quilt back up. "I like your idea to use them as backdrops for photos," Chase told her. "Especially since everyone will be here this Christmas." He paused and added, "Who knows when that will happen again?"

"Oh, Dad . . ." Cat didn't finish, a lump closing off the words in her throat.

Both women knew what was left unspoken: the fact that Chase himself might not be around for many more holidays.

"Tell you what," Sloan said quickly, breaking the awkward silence to address Chase. "As the patriarch, you deserve a photo with every member of the family, one by one, with a different quilt in the background for each. Plus one or two of you alone."

Chase snorted. "The patriarch? Me? Guess I better grow a long white beard and exchange this damned cane for a shepherd's crook."

Jessy had to smile.

Her father-in-law had a twinkle in his eyes as he nodded his agreement, resting a gnarled hand on the quilt Sloan had just folded up. "Use this one for me. It's plain. No fancy stuff."

"You got it."

Chapter 12

With Christmas only four days away, the countdown had begun. The youngsters were a bundle of eagerness. As far as they were concerned, the time couldn't pass fast enough. For those who hadn't finished their shopping, the holiday was approaching way too quickly. But everywhere, smiles abounded, marked by a certain cheeriness that made the season so merry.

Nowhere was it so apparent than at the Homestead, where Cat was busy, with the help of two teenaged girls on their winter break from school, getting the extra bedrooms cleaned and ready for the arriving members of the Calder family. To carry the Christmas spirit a step further, Cat added a holiday candle wreathed with holly to each room, along with childhood pictures of Laura and Quint taken at Christmas time, to their assigned rooms.

After placing a framed photo of Quint on a dresser, she stepped back to assess the dresser top arrangement. Anne Trumbo stuck her head out of the room's adjoining bath.

"Miss Cat, there isn't an extra set of bath towels in here."

"There's some in the laundry room downstairs," Cat remembered. "I'll go get them while you and Sarah finish up here."

When she reached the top of the stairs, she heard the familiar strains of "Jingle Bells" coming from the den and guessed that her father had the radio on. As she started down the steps, she automatically began humming along with the song.

From the den came a slightly flat baritone voice singing, "Bells on bobtails ring, making spirits bright."

Chase was singing! The towels could wait. This she had to see.

She ran lightly the rest of the way down the steps and crossed to the room's open doorway. There was Chase standing at the fireplace, singing away, one hand braced on the head of his cane while he jabbed at the burning logs with a poker.

Cat waited until the final notes of the song died away before speaking. "You're definitely in the holiday mood, Dad."

With the cane for a pivot point he half-turned in surprise, then flashed a smile, eyes twinkling. "And why wouldn't I be? It's nearly Christmas." He returned the poker to its stand. "And a good one it's going to be, too."

Cat smiled in agreement. "It is going to be good to have both Quint and Laura home for Christmas this year. Usually only one or the other can make it."

"Indeed it will be." He hobbled back to his

chair behind the desk. "Do you have the rooms ready for them yet?"

"Almost. I was just on my way to the laundry room to fetch an extra set of towels for Quint and Dallas's bath."

"Better get an extra room ready," he told her.

"Why? Who's coming?"

"I just spoke to Wade a bit ago. He should be here on the twenty-third. The twenty-fourth at the latest. It's liable to be late in the afternoon when he gets here, so I told him to plan on spending the night with us." The twinkle in his eyes grew more pronounced. "I didn't think you'd object to an extra guest, considering that I noticed there was a present under the tree with his name on it."

Cat refused to be self-conscious about it. "You know when I bought that gift for him, I was concerned that I might be presuming too much. Now I'm so glad that I did it, even if it is just a little something." She paused, then asked, "Do you know what I—"

"Quiet." He almost barked the word and swiveled his chair to reach for the volume knob on the radio. Cat had been only vaguely aware of the disc jockeys talking in the background, but her father clearly had one ear tuned to their conversation.

"—being an old Grinch. Everyone wants a white Christmas," one of them declared.

"A white Christmas would be fine, but a winter

storm warning scheduled to blow into eastern Montana by the twenty-fourth! Who wants that?"

"Santa will have some dicey flying conditions, won't he?"

There was more, but Chase snapped the radio off. "We need to call Quint and Laura so they can make sure to get here before the storm does."

"I'll call Quint on my cell while you ring Laura." Cat started out of the room.

Chase called after her. "While you're at it, find Trey. Tell him that I need to see him."

Within an hour both Quint and Laura had been alerted to the forecasted winter storm predicted for Christmas Eve. Both had already begun adjusting their schedules to arrive at the Triple C ahead of it. Twenty minutes later, Trey walked into the den.

"Cat sent a message that you needed to see me."

"Yes." A movement beyond the doorway drew Chase's glance as one of the teenaged girls walked by. "Close the doors."

Trey made a rapid scan of his grandfather's expression, realizing this must be something important, and trying to gauge the seriousness of it. As always, Chase's expression was difficult to read. He closed the doors and crossed to one of the wing-backed chairs.

"Laredo's over at the Shamrock ranch," Chase announced.

Trey drew his head back in surprise. "The Shamrock. What's he doing there?"

"Hiding out. I told him when it was safe for him to come back, I'd send—only you. Go tell him to come home."

"Will do." Trey didn't bother to ask for any explanations. Like others, he knew Laredo's past didn't bear close scrutiny. If Laredo had needed a place to lie low, then he'd had his reasons, and it wasn't important for Trey to know what they were.

"If anyone should ask—and I mean anyone— don't tell them where you're going or why," Chase instructed.

"No problem," Trey assured him.

"Have you heard the forecast?" Chase asked. Trey walked to the door.

He paused in front of the doors. "We're already checking to make sure each camp has extra hay on hand and hauling round bales to all the isolated pastures. After that, we'll just have to wait to see how strong the winds are and whether the cattle start drifting with them."

In short, all was being done that could be done.

A half hour before dinner that night, Trey returned to the Homestead followed by Laredo. Jessy's face lit up when she saw him.

"You're back." She smiled up at Laredo, automatically fitting herself to his side.

"Miss me?"

"Only every day," Jessy admitted with her usual candor.

Chase emerged from the den and saw the two together. "Don't be asking any questions about where's he been, Jessy. For now, that's a secret between Laredo and me."

She laughed. "I won't. Unlike some, I like being surprised on Christmas."

"Good." Chase nodded and continued on his way to the dining room.

Jessy and Laredo followed at a much slower pace. "Have you already been to the Boar's Nest?" she wondered.

"Didn't have time, though it would have been nice to clean up and get a change of clothes."

"We can both go after dinner. I have a surprise to show you," Jessy told him, aware the Christmas hot tub was something he was bound to notice as soon as he got there.

"A surprise, huh?" There was a knowing gleam in his blue eyes. "It wouldn't happen to be—"

She pressed two fingers to his mouth, stopping him from finishing his sentence. "No questions from you either."

He grinned. "Fair enough."

By mid-morning on the twenty-fourth, the skies had already turned a sullen gray, but it was the ominous bank of dark clouds to the northeast that

228

foretold the storm's approach. For the time being the air was still, barely a breath of wind, but Trey wasn't fooled by that. The northeast was the home to what the Sioux Indians called the White Wolf—a howling Arctic blizzard.

Hands thrust deep in the pockets of his sheepskin-lined parka, Trey stood at the window of the office area sectioned off the airstrip's main hangar and watched the sky. Behind him the radio crackled.

"Five miles out on final approach."

Trey spotted the twin-engine cargo plane seconds later, making its descent. Later came the low drone of its engines. Not until its wheels touched down on the ranch's private airstrip did Trey leave the relative warmth of the hangar office.

The plane taxied to a stop on the apron area not far from where Trey waited. By the time Gus Hanson got the chocks tucked behind the wheels, the plane's door swung open, and its flight of steps was lowered. Trey moved forward when Quint ducked through the opening, carrying his young son all bundled in a hooded parka and bulky mittens.

One glimpse of his cousin's high, hard cheekbones and glistening black hair that spoke of his Sioux ancestry and Trey broke into a wide smile. "Welcome home, Quint." He caught hold of Quint's hand and clamped his own onto

Quint's shoulder, in what served as a man-hug. "How was the flight?"

"Not bad."

"Well, I've certainly been on smoother ones," Dallas declared, emerging from the plane, the shiny copper color of her hair sharply contrasted by the dull gray of the fuselage.

Quint turned to offer her a steadying hand while she negotiated the steps. Her grandfather Empty Garner stood framed in the opening behind her, waiting his turn.

"I thought we were on a rodeo. 'Course it might be cause we had such a noisy passenger."

"Had some turbulence," Trey guessed as he gave Dallas a quick hug of greeting.

"It wasn't that bad," Quint insisted. "Especially when you consider that cargo planes aren't exactly famous for giving smooth rides."

"I'd ask why you chose it, but I suspect the reason is somehow connected to your request that I have a pickup and stock trailer waiting for you at the hangar area." Trey hooked a thumb in the direction of the vehicle parked next to his SUV. "Something tells me you didn't ask for it just to haul your luggage and Christmas presents."

"Yes and no," Quint said, being deliberately evasive. "Actually I need it for one special present that I'm delivering at Chase's request."

Trey raised an eyebrow. "What in God's name did he ask you to buy?"

Quint only laughed. "Considering it's for Jake, maybe it's better if you don't know yet."

Gus stepped out of the hangar office and called to Trey. "Laura's pilot just radioed in, asking for landing instructions. Can't be more than ten minutes out."

"Ten minutes." Trey threw a questioning look at Quint. "Do you think we have enough time to get you loaded and dropped off at the Homestead and back up here before her plane lands? If not, I'll have to cram her and Sebastian in the pickup. Which won't exactly thrill my sister."

"She's a Calder. She'll get over it. Still, we might make it. We won't know until we try," Quint replied and transferred his sleepy-eyed son to his wife. "Let's get our luggage loaded."

Before Gus disappeared back inside the hangar, Trey waved to him. "Come give us a hand with the luggage."

As Gus trotted over, Quint suggested, "You might have whoever is driving the pickup back the trailer up to the cargo door. There's a ramp with chutes inside that should reach."

"A ramp? Just what are you hauling?"

"You'll find out after we get all the bags loaded."

With both Empty Garner and Gus to help, they managed all the suitcases and multiple sacks of Christmas gifts in one trip. By the time they had it all loaded in the back of the SUV, the stock trailer was positioned at the plane's cargo door.

Empty climbed into the backseat to wait with Dallas and little Josh while Trey and Quint returned to the plane to unload Jake's Christmas present. Trey took one look at the brown and white speckled calf as it exploded out of its confining transport stall and careened down the chute into the trailer, bucking and bawling the whole way.

"He bought Jake a calf?" Trey turned a dumbfounded look on Quint. "The Triple C has hundreds of them. Why couldn't—"

"None of them are registered Longhorns," Quint informed him, and before Trey could ask the next logical question, added, "Why a Longhorn? That's a question you'll have to take up with Gramps. In the meantime, you wait for Laura and I'll take Dallas and Empty to the house. See you in a bit."

True to his word, Quint pulled up to the hangar area about the time the private jet streaked into view. He climbed out of the passenger seat and joined Trey on the tarmac.

"Good timing."

"For all of us," Quint said and jerked his head at the looming dark clouds. "The White Wolf is inching closer. Probably be here around mid-afternoon."

Trey nodded agreement as the jet swooped onto the runway. The high whine of its engines grew to a roar as they were switched to reverse thrust, and the aircraft slowed. Soon it was taxiing toward them.

Even after the plane rolled to a stop and cut its engines, neither Trey nor Quint approached it until the passenger door opened. A sandy-haired Sebastian stepped out first, his long overcoat hanging open unbuttoned, a plaid scarf looped around his neck. He threw them a saluting wave and glided down the steps, then turned to wait for Laura. As if on cue, she appeared in the opening, wrapped in a full-length sable coat, a matching fur hat covering her blonde head, and paused a beat.

Trey murmured an amused aside to Quint, "My sister, she always likes to make a grand entrance. Married life hasn't changed that about her."

Quint just smiled, fully aware that Trey could poke fun at his twin sibling, but nobody else had better. He stood to one side while the two exchanged an affectionate hug.

"It's good to have you home again, sis," Trey said, and meant it, then teased, "Although that's some carriage your ladyship arrived in."

"It is, isn't it?" she agreed, then declared with typical airiness, "But, since Tara chose to leave us all that money, I decided to take a page out of her book and charter a jet. Eliminate all that security and terminal nonsense you have to deal with when you fly commercial. It cuts a lot of travel time."

"I imagine it does," Trey conceded.

"Besides, this way we could stop over in New York and break up that long flight."

"You were in New York in that coat?" Trey said. "I'm surprised somebody didn't throw paint on you."

"Don't be silly. We stayed at The Pierre. I saw more extravagant coats than this one there."

"I'll take your word for it," he said and stepped back as she moved to greet Quint with a hug.

"You beat us here," she chided in mock reproof. "I thought I'd be the one waiting to welcome you."

"We landed about fifteen minutes ago," Quint told her. "I've already dropped Dallas at the house. They're all just waiting for you now."

"I can't wait to see everybody again." The earnest words were barely out of her mouth when she noticed the pickup and stock trailer and arched an accusing look at Trey. "Is that your idea of a joke? A stock trailer to haul all my luggage in? I know you think I pack way too many things, but I'm never sure what I'll need."

"I wish I'd thought of using it for that," Trey began, only to be interrupted by the calf letting out a bellow.

"The trailer's already occupied," she realized.

"I don't think your luggage would fare too well, sharing the space with Jake's Christmas present," Quint remarked.

Laura looked to Trey for an explanation.

"Gramps bought him a registered Longhorn calf that's going to grow up to be a bad-tempered, bondy-shouldered, speckled bull with horns wider than Old Captain's."

"What was he thinking?" Laura mirrored Trey's earlier astonishment.

"Damned if I know," Trey admitted. "It's too cold to keep standing out here talking about it, though. Come on," he said to Quint. "Let's start unloading her luggage. Lord knows, it'll probably take two trips to get it all."

With the two families arriving so closely on the heels of each other, it created a noisy, confusing scene: everyone talking at once, luggage stacked everywhere, coats temporarily piled on chairs to be collected later. The initial flurry of greetings and chatter had barely subsided when it all started again as they attempted to sort through the stacks and carry everything upstairs to the proper rooms.

Any semblance of normalcy didn't return until they all gathered in the dining room for the noon meal. But the conversation was much more lively than usual, with questions and answers flowing back and forth as each tried to catch up on the happenings in the others' lives. It wasn't until the meal was over and the women were carrying the dirty dishes to the kitchen while the men lingered at the table over the coffee that anyone noticed the snowflakes drifting past the window.

Trey nudged Quint's arm and nodded to the

snow. "You've been in Texas so long you've lost your Montana weather eye. The White Wolf moved faster than you thought."

"Not much of a wind yet," Quint observed.

"What's that?" Chase asked, missing the first part of their low exchange.

"It's started snowing." Trey saw the way Chase snapped his head around to look outside. "It isn't heavy yet."

"And not much of a wind either," Quint added, "judging by the way those flakes are falling."

"But it's coming," Chase stated grimly and grasped his cane to push himself up from the chair and walk over to look out the window.

When Cat re-entered the dining room, she immediately noticed his chair was vacant and saw him standing at the window. Guessing he was about to retreat to his den, she asked, "Would you like me to take a pot of coffee to the den for you, Dad?"

When he failed to respond, she walked over to his side, thinking he probably hadn't heard with everyone else talking. She touched his arm, drawing his glance. "Coffee in den?"

"Might as well," he replied with marked indifference and turned to stare out the window again. That's when Cat noticed the white flakes.

"It's started snowing already," she murmured.

"The brunt of the storm hasn't hit yet. He still has time to get here."

She didn't have to ask whom he meant. Wade was the only one either of them was expecting. "He could," she repeated, except she knew he wasn't due until later in the afternoon. And the storm's fury wasn't likely to hold off that long. She started to tell Chase that, but one look at her father's face and she realized he already knew it.

"He'll have sense enough to stay somewhere if the weather's bad." Cat didn't realize she'd spoken the thought until Chase replied.

"Of course he will."

That also meant he wouldn't make it for Christmas. Before any sense of disappointment could take hold, Cat lifted her head, reminding herself that seeing Wade after Christmas was just as good.

She turned back toward the table as Dallas came in from the kitchen, stopped, looked around the room, then shot a look at Quint. "Where's Josh? It's time for his nap."

"I thought he was with you." Quint pushed his chair back.

"I just saw Jake going toward the living room," Sebastian volunteered.

"Josh probably isn't far behind," Dallas concluded, already moving toward the living room.

"A lot of places in a house this size, aren't there, Trey?" Chase tapped the back of his chair with the cane, then looked to Empty Garner.

"Cat's going to bring a pot of coffee to the den. Why don't you join me? It's bound to be a bit quieter there."

"Sounds good." Empty got out of his chair to follow him. "I noticed you had a set of Longhorns on the mantel in there."

Cat caught Trey's eye and smiled. Both knew Empty was about to be regaled with the story of Old Captain and that first herd a Calder had trailed north to Montana.

From somewhere in the living room came a whiny protest, "No sleep, Mama. No sleep."

"Somebody doesn't want to take a nap," Cat guessed.

"Sounds a bit like Jake when he was that age," Trey recalled.

"Something tells me he won't be any more successful than Jake was at getting out of it," Cat said and collected the empty coffee cups left on the table, carrying them off to the kitchen.

Josh's nap proved to be a short one. By two o'clock he was back downstairs, full of energy and raring to unleash it. With the noon dishes all done, everyone had congregated in the living room. Outside, the snowfall was heavier and the wind had picked up, the first rattling gusts hitting the windows.

Chase was in his favorite armchair, which was now flanked by the two wingbacked chairs from the den. Empty Garner sat in one while Laredo occupied the other. Jessy and Sloan were on the couch with Laura seated between them, looking at the photo album Laura had brought with her, full of pictures showing her latest renovations at Crawford Hall. Quint and Trey lounged on the love seat, their feet propped on the leather ottoman while Dallas sat sideways on one of its arms, keeping an eye on her young son, who was being taught how to roll a ball by Cat. Jake was poking through the new presents under the tree, searching for any with his name on it.

After closely examining the tag on a fairly good-sized square one, Jake picked it up and carried it over to Trey. "Is this one mine, Dad?"

Trey glanced at the gift tag and shook his head. "Sorry. Better put it back."

"But it gots a J on it," he argued.

"J for Josh, not Jake," Trey explained.

Jake heaved a dramatic sigh of regret and carried it back to the piles of presents that now encircled the Christmas tree. Trey watched to make sure he returned it, then slid a glance at Laredo.

"I heard you got to open your Christmas present early when you came back to the Boar's Nest yesterday, Laredo," he remarked.

"A hot tub is a little big to hide anywhere," Laredo countered.

"And impossible to wrap," Jessy added, looking up from the photo album.

"Jessy did put a big red bow on it that was pretty hard to miss." His voice was strongly laced with both amusement and affection.

"Did you test the water?" Quint leaned forward, to look around Dallas at Laredo.

"Damned right I did," Laredo declared.

"You should have seen him," Jessy declared. "Up to his neck, steam all around and wearing his cowboy hat and smoking a big cigar."

"Had to wear my hat," Laredo drawled. "I needed to keep my head from getting cold."

"Too bad you didn't have your camera, Mom." Laura smiled in regret. "That picture would have been pinned up on every bulletin board on the Triple C."

"Might have been a bit hard for Jessy to take a picture," Laredo pointed out, an impish gleam lighting his blue eyes, "considering she was in the tub, too."

As gleeful laughter broke out, Jessy smiled along with them and shook her head in mock reproach. "You just had to tell 'em."

"I think they would have figured it out," Laredo said with a wink.

"Now that picture would have been priceless," Quint stated. "No doubt about it."

Jake came running up and threw himself across Trey's legs. "Can I open one of my presents early. 'Redo got to."

"Nope."

"Aww please." He dragged the word out in a soulful plea.

"You heard your father, Jake," Sloan put in, adding her weight to Trey's refusal.

He swung around to scowl at her, arms akimbo. "How come?"

Sloan fell back on the tried and true answer. "Because we said so." Jake's shoulders slumped in defeat.

About then Josh found rolling a ball on the floor much too tame, and gave it a swat, sending the ball flying into the den. With a squeal of glee, he took off toward the dining room at his fastest version of a run.

"Josh, come back here!" Dallas pushed off the love seat's arm to go after him. But Cat was already on her feet. "I'll bring him back."

As she started toward the dining room, Jake took off for the stairs. Trey sat up, and swiveled around to watch him race up the steps.

"Why's he going upstairs?" He eyed Sloan, a curious and wary line creasing his forehead.

"Who knows?" She shrugged and redirected her attention to the photo album on Laura's lap.

"Quint," Chase began, turning a thoughtful look on his grandson. "Did you ever notice the hair color that boy of yours has? In a certain light, it's as orange as a carrot. If he was any smaller, a rabbit might try to eat him."

"Bright, isn't it?" Empty agreed. "It'll darken up as he gets older. Dallas's did."

Chase ran an appraising glance over the rich copper sheen of her hair, and decided, after some consideration. "That'd be all right."

Laredo gave her a thumbs up. "You passed inspection."

Cat reappeared, shooing a giggling Josh in front of her. As if on cue, Jake clumped down the stairs with something in his hand. No one had a clear view of it until he reached the bottom.

"What are you doing with that rope, Jake?" Trey immediately wanted to know.

"I'm gonna use it t'catch Josh the next time he runs off," Jake asserted, extremely pleased with himself for coming up with the solution.

"Oh, no, you're not, young man," Sloan said with a quick shake of her head. "Ropes aren't for catching people. Only horses and cattle."

"But it'd be good practice, Mom."

"Bring me the rope, Jake." Trey snapped his fingers and motioned to him. Feet dragging and the corners of his mouth turned down, Jake walked over and laid the coiled rope in his father's outstretched hand.

"What goes around, always comes around," Chase declared, looking directly at Trey and Quint. "And seeing that reminds me of you two when you were his age, always up to something and inches away from being in trouble. It's amazing how parents get to raise a replica of themselves."

"So that's where Jake gets all his wild ideas." Sloan nodded in sudden understanding while sliding Trey a teasing look.

Abruptly Chase cocked his head at a listening angle. "Did you hear that?"

"Hear what?" Laredo asked, coming alert.

"A noise. I thought it came from outside," Chase replied, then glanced at Cat. "You're already up. Go see if anyone's there."

"I think you're hearing things, Dad. But I'll go check." Like him, Cat knew there was an off chance that Wade might have arrived. The possibility had her walking a little more quickly to the entryway.

Chapter 13

When Cat looked out the window next to the front door, the view was obscured by the heavy snowfall, driven by blustering winds. Through the wintry veil, she could just make out the darker shape of the big-timbered barn in the distance. But there was nothing else, no vehicle and no human.

Any sense of disappointment she felt quickly gave way to relief. Cat didn't want to think about Wade being out in this storm. Just hearing the muted howl of the wind almost made her shudder at the thought.

She returned to the living room. "It must have been the wind you heard, Dad," she told him, then included the others. "It's really getting bad out there. I can just barely make out the shape of the old barn. Visibility is down to less than a hundred feet. I'm glad you all arrived when you did."

"And so say all of us." Sebastian raised his glass in a toasting gesture that offered a whole-hearted agreement with her sentiment.

"Personally," Laura began, "I'm rather glad that we're suddenly in the midst of a full-fledged blizzard. It snows occasionally in England, but the storms don't have the violence that Montana can dish out. I've missed that a little."

"Leave it to you to find it exciting," Trey

muttered in a mixture of exasperation and resignation.

"Please, no lectures on the losses the Triple C could suffer from this," she countered. "I'm well aware of all the problems this will bring. But the storm's here. There's nothing anyone can do to stop it, so I'm choosing to enjoy it."

Trey started to reply, but Jessy broke in. "Let's not start bickering, you two."

Sloan supported her by changing the subject. "Dallas, would you like to look at Laura's pictures of the restoration work they've been doing at Crawford Hall? We're finished with the album."

Banding with them, Dallas readily agreed. "Yes, I would."

Laura closed the album and handed it to her.

"What's the next project you're going to tackle, Laura?" Sloan asked to keep the conversation going.

"Face it, Trey." Laura grinned at her twin brother. "We're outnumbered. We'll have to do our squabbling when we're alone."

"Like always." He smiled back at her.

"Your next project," Sloan persisted, slicing a silencing look at Trey.

"I have nothing major planned." Laura paused and made eye contact with Sebastian, a smile edging the corners of her mouth. "Just some minor redecorating of the bedroom next to ours."

"Really," Jessy said with some surprise. "I thought you just did that one last year."

"We did," Laura admitted, then paused and glanced again at Sebastian.

He turned his hands in a palms-up gesture, then left the choice to her. "This is as good a time as any to tell them."

"Tell us what?" Now Cat's curiosity was piqued.

"That we're converting that bedroom into a nursery." She said it with all the calmness of someone commenting on the weather, then laughed when her words registered on the faces of her family.

"You're going to have a baby." Jessy was the first to actually say it, in a stunned but happy murmur.

After that everyone chimed in, flooding both soon-to-be parents with congratulations and questions. Foremost among the latter was "When?"

"End of July, first of August," Laura told them.

"How long have you known?" Jessy gazed at her daughter, still marveling over the prospect of her daughter becoming a mother.

"A couple months," Laura admitted. "I wanted to wait until we were here to tell everyone. Our own Christmas surprise."

"Well, I'm surprised, that's for sure," Jessy declared.

"Not me." Trey grinned at his sister. "You've always been highly competitive. You couldn't stand that Quint and I were already one up on you."

With a defiant and faintly laughing toss of her head, Laura didn't bother to deny it. "Not for long, you won't be, because I'm going to go you one better."

"You're having twins." Trey stared at her in amazement.

"Naturally. If I'm going to lose my figure anyway, I might as well provide the proverbial heir and a spare while I'm at it." Laura was clearly reveling in their stunned but happy reaction.

"You're having boys," Sloan breathed in surprise.

"We are," Laura confirmed.

Chase's brows pulled together. "You already know?"

"With today's technology, it's amazing how quickly they can tell these days, Gramps," she said, then turned to Jessy, smiling. "In fact, that's one of your presents under the tree. Framed pictures of the digital sonogram showing the two little rascals."

"I can hardly wait to see it," Jessy declared, then laughed. "I sound like Jake."

"Now you have to start picking out names," Dallas murmured. "It was hard enough deciding on a name for one. You have to choose two."

Laura slid a look at Chase. "I already know I want to call one of them Benteen after my side of the family. We still haven't settled on one from Sebastian's side."

Laredo gave Chase's arm a light poke. "And you think it's noisy with two great-grandsons running around. Imagine what it'll be like with four."

A harrumphing grunt came from him. "Remind me to ask for a pair of earplugs next Christmas," he said as Jake ducked behind his chair to get away from Josh. Undeterred, Josh dropped onto all fours and crawled after him.

In his haste to elude the toddler, Jake ran into the end table. The lamp teetered for an instant before Laredo reached out to steady it. By then Jake had bounced off a corner of the sofa.

"Did you hear that thump?" Chase swung his head around to stare in the direction of the entryway.

"That was Jake bumping into the sofa," Cat told him.

"No, not that. It came from outside," he insisted, scowling his impatience with her.

"Then you probably heard the wind," she began.

"Dammit, I'm old, not deaf." Chase grabbed up his cane and levered himself out of the chair. "And I know the difference between the sound of the wind and someone outside."

"Dad, there is no one out there." But she was talking to his back as he used his cane to stomp out of the living room. Now totally irritated with him, Cat quickly brushed past her father on her way to the entrance. "Go back and sit down. I'll go look for you."

"Take a good look while you're at it," Chase called after her, slowing his headlong pace. "Don't just go through the motion of glancing out the window, thinking I'm going to be satisfied with that."

"As if I can see anything the way that snow's blowing," Cat muttered to herself as she crossed to the window, hearing the way the wind battered itself against the house.

Just as she reached the window and leaned closer to look through the panes, the front door burst open. Thinking it had been blown by the wind, Cat reached out to grab it, averting her face from the swirling rush of wind and snow. At the last second she caught a glimpse of a snow-spattered figure stepping across the threshold.

"Sorry." Wade's voice reached out to her. "The wind ripped the door right out of my hand."

He caught hold of it and shouldered it closed, while she stood staring at him in disbelief. He turned toward her, a wet glisten to his face from the melting flakes.

"Dad said he heard someone, but I didn't believe him," Cat admitted, still finding it hard to believe her eyes. "I didn't think anyone would venture out in this storm."

"I thought I had a chance to make it before the snow hit. It didn't work out that way." He tugged off his gloves and stuffed them in the pockets of his wool coat.

"You should have stopped somewhere." But now that he was here, Cat was glad he hadn't. And it showed in her face as she moved to help him off with his coat.

"By the time that occurred to me, I was already past the point of no return. And stopping in the middle of nowhere didn't seem too wise either."

"You could have ended up in a ditch somewhere." She made quick work of hanging up his coat.

"I nearly did. More than once."

"It's a damned good thing you didn't," Chase stated, announcing his presence.

Cat was about to take issue with the gruffness of her father's voice when she saw the beam of approval and pride in his regard of Wade. He sounded gruff, she realized, because he was overcome with emotion. She wondered if Wade could see it. The way he smiled back at Chase told her he did.

"I told you I'd be here in time," Wade said simply.

Chase nodded in approval. "And you're a man of your word."

"I am." Wade reached inside his jacket and pulled out an envelope. "Here it is. Signed, sealed, and delivered." He passed it to Chase.

For a moment, Chase simply held the envelope, his gaze fixed on it. Then his chest lifted with a deep breath and he raised his head. "Thank you." His low voice trembled with a wealth of emotion.

Jessy came striding out of the living room, then halted when she saw the man facing Chase. "Wade. When I heard Chase talking to someone, I thought it was one of the hands, bringing me word of—With a storm like this, it could be anything. Don't tell me, you drove through it?" she said as Laredo wandered up behind her.

"For about the last fifty miles." Wade nodded. "Which took me almost two hours to cover."

"I guess you know how lucky you are without me telling you." She gave a marveling shake of her head. More footsteps signaled the arrival of Quint and Trey. "There's a fire going in the living room. You'd better come get warm."

"Not yet," Chase asserted, checking any movement toward the living room. He made a slow turn, something in his body language conveying a desire for all to remain. His solemn expression added weight to the moment.

Unconsciously Cat held her breath, sensing he was about to make an important announcement. She was without a clue as to what it might be. Or what Wade's involvement in all this was. Judging by the attentive way Jessy, Laredo, Trey, and Quint waited for him to speak, they shared her awareness of the moment.

Strangely, when he spoke, all Chase said was—"This is for you, Laredo." He extended the envelope to him.

Bewilderment flickered across Laredo's face. He hesitated, then stepped forward to take the envelope. He looked at it, but made no move to open it as he lifted a questioning look to Chase.

Something Cat could only call affection gentled Chase's hard, lined face, his eyes warm with understanding.

"Maybe I should have said the document inside is for Scott Ludlow, Jr," Chase said.

Immediately Trey took a backward step and motioned for the others still in the living room to join them. And there was a sharpening of Laredo's questioning look. "How—"

Chase cut across his words. "Does it matter?" A near smile softened the line of his mouth. His glance flicked briefly to the onlookers, taking note of Sloan's arrival, followed closely by that of Dallas, Laura, and Sebastian. Then again his attention centered on Laredo.

"In that envelope, you'll find a full pardon from the Mexican government. Any and all previous charges against you have been wiped from their records."

An audible gasp came from Sloan. She tried to smother it with her hand as she looked up at Trey, who smiled back. Jessy laid a quick hand on Laredo's arm, her expression alive with happiness for him.

Laredo wore a stunned look. "How did you manage that?"

"With Wade's help," Chase replied.

Cat felt a swelling of pride in her chest. Discreetly she slipped her hand into Wade's, linking fingers with him, pleased and proud of the role he had played in this.

Deeply moved, Laredo shook his head. "I don't know what to say."

"After all you have done for this family, this is the least we can do for you," Chase replied. "Merry Christmas."

"Open it," Jessy urged in a low voice.

Laredo obliged and removed the official looking paper, holding it so Jessy could see it too. "Scott Ludlow," he murmured. "I don't even know who that is anymore."

"There's nothing to stop you from legally changing your name to Laredo Smith if that's what you want," Chase pointed out.

"I guess not." Laredo nodded and glanced sideways at Jessy. "There's no reason we can't get yours legally changed at the same time."

Her mouth opened in surprise, a telltale shimmer of tears welling in her eyes. When she failed to say anything, Trey spoke up, "That sounds like a proposal to me, Mom."

"And in front of witnesses, too," Laura added.

Jessy laughed softly. "It had better be one, because I'm accepting it."

Holding the document in one hand, Laredo wrapped an arm around Jessy and held her tightly to his side before planting one hard, quick kiss on her mouth. Both looked a little self-conscious when a mix of cheers and clapping erupted around them.

"Glad to see you're going to make an honest woman of her, Laredo." Chase nodded his approval.

"Only because you made an honest one of me." Respect and gratitude was in his look.

Jake ran into the entryway, looking around. "What's everybody yelling about? Did Santa come?"

"You might say that." Laredo grinned.

"Where'd he go?" Jake turned and spotted Wade. "Greypa, he was here!" He looked at Chase with open-eyed wonder. "He brought Aunt Cat's husband for her!"

Chuckling, Chase ruffled the top of his head. "He certainly did."

Center Point Publishing
600 Brooks Road ● PO Box 1
Thorndike ME 04986-0001 USA

(207) 568-3717

US & Canada:
1 800 929-9108
www.centerpointlargeprint.com